WHEN NEXT WE LOVE

*Also by Heather Graham
in Large Print:*

Lord of the Wolves
Queen of Hearts
Spirit of the Season

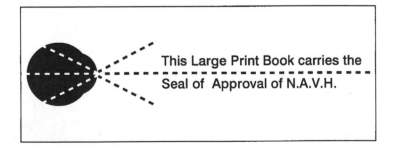

WHEN NEXT WE LOVE

Heather Graham

*Large
Print
c1*

Thorndike Press • Thorndike, Maine

Published in 2000 by arrangement with Leisure Books, a division of Dorchester Publishing Co., Inc.

Thorndike Press Large Print Famous Authors Series.

The tree indicium is a trademark of Thorndike Press.

The text of this Large Print edition is unabridged.
Other aspects of the book may vary from the original edition.

Set in 16 pt. Plantin.

Printed in the United States on permanent paper.

Library of Congress Cataloging-in-Publication Data

Graham, Heather.
    When next we love / Heather Graham.
       p.   cm.
    ISBN 0-7862-2522-X (lg. print : hc : alk. paper)
    1. Hurricanes — Fiction. 2. Florida — Fiction.
  3. Widows — Fiction. 4. Large type books. I. Title
  PS3557.R198 W47   2000
    813′.54—dc21   00-025195

For E. D. Graham,
who taught us dreams could be real.

Prologue

She had known him for years, yet she didn't know him at all. They had been the best of friends, the worst of enemies.

But tonight it didn't matter. There was no past, and of course, as only she knew, there would be no future.

Just the night.

And she hadn't even planned it. Things were simply working out that way, and she was powerless to call a halt. She didn't want to call a halt. In the back of her mind she knew she had wanted him for an eternity. But consciously, even with the surrounding magic and music — and the fair amount of liquor she had consumed! — she would never admit that it was really him she wanted, or that want had a deep root in her emotions involving him.

And it wasn't really *her* who wanted *him*. It was the exotic belly dancer of her disguise who was falling in love with the handsome and noble King Arthur of his whimsical attire.

And he didn't know who she really was.

The opportunity was too good to miss. He would never know. The rinse had successfully colored her hair black; the blue-tinged contact lenses completely hid her own eye color. Heavily applied bronze-toned pancake makeup had taken her normally cream complexion to a much darker hue, while carefully drawn lines and heavy shadows of dark rich color had given her eyes a mysterious, Far East cast. The lower portion of her face was misted by a veil of fine silk gauze. Perpetually leaning to the slim side, the trauma she had endured over the past few months had taken its toll upon her weight, and her costume, floating and flaring over curves now highlighted by gaunt shadows, did the rest to assure her complete change of person so that not even her mother would have recognized her.

It had started as a lark. She had intended to announce her identity later in the evening. Then it had all gone so well . . . of course, it was understandable. She hadn't seen any of them in a very long time.

He had singled her out immediately. Their eyes had met across the room, and his had swept over her with astute appreciation. And before she knew it, she was in his arms.

And it felt so good, so *right!*

Had he been King Arthur in truth, Lancelot would have never stood a chance. He was everything wonderful — tall, strong, arrogantly masculine, and yet unceasingly tender.

When he suggested that they leave, she didn't blink an eye. She didn't bother to think about the deceit she was weaving; it didn't occur to her. She was caught in her own fantasy, unmindful of the repercussions that could follow. To her, they were strangers who had known one another forever, timeless lovers, partners in a dance that had just begun.

She vaguely noted that Pinocchio and a Dresden doll were discussing the London Company as they neared the pair, lamenting the death of the lead guitarist, Richard Tremayne.

"They're still on top, though," Pinocchio said admiringly. "I always did say that Derek Mallory was the talent behind the group."

"Yes, but Tremayne was exceptional," the Dresden doll commented.

"Umm — a genius," interrupted a Fruit of the Loom grape. "I hear his wife helped him, too. Has anyone seen her? They say she clammed up, wouldn't see or talk to anyone."

"I invited Leigh," Pinocchio said. "I guess she couldn't make it."

"Maybe she knew Derek would be here," someone snickered. "And he knows —"

"He knows what?"

The demand came curtly from King Arthur. She was forced to stop and snap into reality for a moment as he challenged the group.

"Nothing, nothing," was the mumbled reply.

"Leigh Tremayne is a sweet lady," Pinocchio said sincerely.

"She was my best friend's wife," King Arthur returned in a deadly voice that held definite warning. "I don't like to hear gossip about either of them. Richard is dead. Let him rest in peace."

"We all loved Richard," the Dresden doll said softly, easing the tension that had risen. Then she smiled at Arthur. "You're not leaving, are you?"

"Yes," Arthur said. "But thanks for a super party."

Pinocchio glanced longingly at the belly dancer by King Arthur's side. "You can't leave! We still haven't figured out the true identity of your lovely lady here."

"Neither have I!" Arthur chuckled, grinning at her. "But I intend to."

10

She almost panicked. They were scrutinizing her too intently. But she held on to her composure and smiled, then affected a superb Irish accent learned from a doting grandparent. "You'll have to think on it then, friends, for we are indeed leaving. But I add my thanks for a terrific night."

They were watched as they left the party. He, because he would always draw attention by the authority of his regal size and unusual eyes, she because she was simply stunning, an enchantress tonight. The eyes that observed their departure mirrored many human emotions — admiration, wistfulness, curiosity, envy, and downright jealousy.

They were barely conscious of the stares that followed them. He was too enamored; she was too busy fighting her nervousness and pushing all the little fears that confronted her to the back of her mind.

He'll never know! she repeated over and over to herself. And finally, she was convinced.

And so began the fantasy, the most wonderful night of her life.

It was slow and easy and wonderful. He took her to a house he was borrowing from a friend for the weekend nestled among the magnolia trees, and they listened to the gentle strains of classical music before the light radiating from the mellow fire. They talked for hours, as the embers cast their dying glow, and she was relieved as the shadows became deeper, and the darkness became the protector of her identity. Even after he had asked her to remove her veil, he learned nothing of her, nor did he press. He too seemed to know that the night was mystical, a fantasy spun with silken thread.

Their talking tapered into comfortable silence. He rose slowly and offered her his hand. By mute agreement she trustingly accepted him, and when she, too, was standing, he swept her as effortlessly as stardust into his arms and lay her tenderly on the bed, where he began to disrobe her with loving reverence.

She was naked now, more susceptible than ever to discovery. But she was lost in an endless field of longing and desire, totally absorbed by the magnificent male form before her, framed in a silhouette by the pale light of the moon like a true king. His lips touched her flesh and created a wildfire, his hands worshipped her, his limbs, against hers, demanded and possessed. He leased and tormented, feathery light, soft as a breeze. Then his tongue traced the mound of a firm breast and he drew his teeth over a hardening nipple. She moaned low in her throat and her fingers sank into his hair. Gentleness was lost in a swirling, urgent vortex of passion as darkness surrounded them. He whispered husky words to her, words of hunger, of thirst, of sweetness, of awe. He would never have his fill of her.

And she whispered back. Shyly at first, then boldly as she learned she held the same captivating power over him that he did over her. She did, in fact, learn much that night, for he had not lied. He could not drink his full of her soft enchantment. He possessed her as she had never been possessed before, loved her with a beauty she had never imagined. Through the night she marveled at the wonder of giving herself to such a man, of being so completely his. He demanded, he took, and he gave her ecstasy, a ceaseless cloud of sensual adoration and pleasure.

Too soon the dawn broke across the heavens. She awoke with a start to find herself entwined with him, her head resting on his golden-haired chest. Pain raged through her mind with the acuteness of a cruel stabbing. It was over. Carefully, very carefully so as not to waken her sleeping king, she disengaged herself and quickly redonned her costume. The contact lenses were cutting her eyes like a thousand slivers, but she didn't dare remove them until she was far away. She scampered to the door, but stopped. She had to go back. Just for a moment. Just to kiss his sleep-eased brow one more time.

Her lips touched his skin, then she backed away. His eyes were beginning to flicker. She made it to the door before he awoke and called for her to stop. Begged, demanded. But he knew that she was fleeing. "I'll find you!" he assured her, stumbling for his pants.

"No," she said, and her voice was torn with sadness. "You don't know where to look."

Then she was gone, racing away, plummeting back to undeniable reality. She knew he chased her, but the gods of fantasy were with her. Like the magic created, she disappeared into thin air.

Well, actually, she disappeared into a city cab. But it made no difference. She was gone to him forever.

Because she was a real woman, and he despised the real woman who she was.

Chapter One

Leigh Tremayne shrugged away the chill that assailed her as an unattached voice demanded her name and business after her Audi pulled to a halt in front of the massive iron gate. It wasn't really the voice that bothered her, she realized. She had been to Derek's Star Island estate before and knew what to expect. What was disturbing her, she admitted, was that she was coming closer and closer to the inevitable — her meeting with Derek.

"It's Mrs. Tremayne," she called irritably. "And you'll have to ask your boss what my business is!"

The gate rolled silently open. For a moment she merely stared at it, her fingers frozen on the wheel of her car. She was suddenly panicking, wishing she had never agreed to come. Then she pushed such ridiculous notions aside and turned the key in the ignition. There was no reason for her not to come; there was no reason for her to fear an encounter with Derek Mallory.

She drove slowly up the gravel driveway and past the manicured lawns, unconsciously smoothing back a wispy tendril of light auburn hair. Acutely aware that there was a good possibility that she was being observed by an electronic eye, she made no attempt to check her appearance. Besides, Richard had once assured her — in the days before he had begun to find fault — that her beauty lay in her "classic nobility of presence." And at twenty-seven she had come to an age when she was capable of assessing herself objectively. She might not be a great beauty, but she was an attractive woman. Almost elegant at times, thanks to the sophistication Richard had laboriously drilled into her. And today she had drawn on every natural asset and every grain of hauteur learned from her late husband. Her copper hair was knotted simply on her head beneath the rim of her low-angled beige hat; her large hazel eyes were subtly highlighted by blended green and brown shadows; her "classic" cheekbones were pronounced by a slight touch of blush.

As she crawled lithely from the car, she casually straightened her beige skirt. She had chosen the outfit, and the three-inch heels despite her slender five-nine frame, for a businesslike and aloof effect. Derek certainly hadn't called her to renew an old friendship. He had made his opinion of her quite clear at Richard's funeral, and they hadn't parted on the best of terms.

Derek, although he didn't say it in so many words, blamed her for the wasteful demise of his friend and partner, Richard Tremayne, undoubtedly one of the finest musicians of the twentieth century. The world mourned Richard sincerely while it seemed to Derek that his widow did not.

But what Derek didn't realize, she thought wryly, was that she had mourned the loss of her husband long before his death. And she had loved him. She had given him her heart, soul, and mind and catered to him completely until she began to lose her own existence in the shadow of his growing tantrums and demands. Then she awoke one day with the bitter and sad assimilation of the truth. Richard loved her in his way, but not enough to grant her the individual devotion of a normal marriage partner. Toward the end he cruelly pointed out that she should be grateful just for the privilege of being his wife. He kept her well; she could have anything in the world. He had literally given her fame and fortune. His laughter when she tried to explain that she didn't want the world but a stable home and family had been the final straw. She had filed for divorce, but Richard's untimely death had left her a widow instead of a "Ms."

The shrill cry of a mockingbird startled her into realizing that she had been staring blankly at the whitewashed facade of Derek's deco mansion. Shaking herself sternly, she climbed the five tile steps of the curved outer doorway and briskly clanged the heavy brass knocker. She was happy now, meeting each day with cheerful anticipation. She had mourned, but the past, with all its good and bad, belonged in its proper perspective. And if Derek Mallory intended to tear down her present complacency with accusations and disapproval, she would be back out the door before she ever sat down.

"Come in, please, Mrs. Tremayne."

Leigh was greeted by Derek's staid and proper butler, an English import like his Waterford crystal. Although Derek and the group spent most of their time in the States, they still considered Great Britain their home and often liked elements of "home" around them. Leigh also knew that the popular conception that the group had risen from the slums of Liverpool was absurdly far from the truth. Each of the five original members of the band had been born to affluent families. Derek, in fact, would one day be Lord Mallory.

"Thank you, James," she told the austere butler. A slightly wicked smile curved her lips. It always amazed her that James, so amazingly dignified and correct, could consistently maintain his rigid discipline of manner amidst the frequent cacophony of his employer's world. "How have you been?"

"Fine, madam, thank you," James replied without a twitch of his countenance. "Now if you'll follow me, please, I'll take you to Mr. Mallory. He's been expecting you, you know."

"Yes, I know," Leigh said smoothly, but James was moving down the cathedral-domed hallway before the words were out of her mouth. She hurried after him, listening to the sharp click of her heels on the Venetian tile of the floor. James was leading her to Derek's large office, a room where he carried out his business affairs and also kept a perfectly tuned grand piano so that he could work whenever the impulse came to him.

James swung open a set of varnished oak double doors, and Leigh stopped abruptly behind him, her eyes drawn to the man at the cherry-wood desk.

Derek was casually seated. His long, jean-clad legs were stretched on top of the desk, crossed at the ankle. A pair of Adidas sneakers adorned his feet, a simple navy tank top exposed more of his broad, golden-haired chest than it covered. His sturdy tanned hands and incredibly long fingers were engaged in holding a ledger and scribbling upon it. His handsome features — high arched brows, deep golden-brown eyes, long aquiline nose, and beard-fringed, sensual mouth — were taut, tense, and engrossed, as if the ledger before him posed infinite problems. At the sound of their approach, he glanced up sharply, his gaze falling quickly from James to Leigh, a dark, fathomless gaze that seemed to strike her with the force of a physical blow, divest her of chic clothing down to the vulnerable flesh, even go beyond the flesh and bare the terrible beating of her heart to open view. How ridiculous! she admonished herself. Cowardly whimsy. Derek couldn't possibly see a thing except a well-dressed young woman.

"Mr. Mallory, Mrs. Tremayne," James announced unnecessarily. He made a clipped goose step and disappeared down the hall.

"Hello, Derek," Leigh said coolly, striding into the room with what she hoped was assurance.

He rose slowly, almost insolently, from his relaxed pose, towering several inches over her despite her own regal height in heels. A shaft of light streamed in from the huge bay windows, highlighting his hair, his beard, and rippled chest to reddish gold as he reached out a hand to take hers, enveloping its fine-boned smoothness in a firm grip. Leigh struggled inwardly to prevent her facial muscles from forming a wince. She was experiencing a far worse reaction than she had expected. It felt as if the long fingers that held her so lightly were charged with electricity, sending shock waves of heat through her entire system. She withdrew her hand as quickly as she could after his slow return of, "Hello, Leigh," dismayed to note the flash of amusement that flickered through his golden-brown eyes at her obvious haste.

"Sit down, will you," he suggested cordially, indicating a comfortable straight-backed but thickly padded chair opposite the desk. She silently acquiesced, taking the opportunity to study him covertly from beneath the shade of her downcast, fluffy lashes.

Derek was undeniably possessed of an innate, animalistic charm. It was something he had a vague acceptance of, like his thick, shaggy hair or deep, compelling eyes. He was superbly built, sinewed but slender, his height belying his true strength and breadth. Powerful, taut shoulders tapered to a steel-flat waist and trim hips and long, well-muscled thighs. Yet his sensuality was not a physical thing, not in that sense. It was part of his languorous movements, his shrewd eyes, his deceptive conviviality. Derek was like a cobra. A woman could find herself hypnotized by those magnetic eyes, lulled by that sleek, fluid grace, then suddenly struck, the victim of a swift and venomous attack. A woman could, if she allowed herself to be vulnerable. And vulnerable, Leigh swore silently, she would never be. In the early days of her marriage she had adored him. Her husband's best friend had become her own. Even then she had been acutely aware of his devastating sexuality. But in those days she had considered herself immune. Her equally charming and talented husband demanded her complete concentration. And then of course Derek would never have dreamed of touching her. Since Leigh was his best friend's wife, Leigh knew that

Derek would rather die than touch her.

But they had been close. For a time, very close. When things began going wrong, Leigh reached for him. And that was when she began to despise him. He turned on her coldly, accusing her of being heartless and mercenary, a frigid, uncaring wife.

Sustained by her memories, she stiffened rigidly in the chair and stared up at Derek imperially. He was now standing before the desk, leaning haphazardly against it, scrutinizing her as she had been him, except openly.

"Why did you ask me here?" she snapped bluntly.

"I wanted to see you," he returned immediately, undaunted by her antagonistic tone.

"Obviously!" she drawled with tart sarcasm. "Why?"

He grinned easily. "My, my!" he mocked. "The ever-sweet, conniving little wife did turn into a waspish widow. Defensive and suspicious. Why not take this at face value? Why not believe that I was simply concerned for your welfare?"

She grinned back with equal malice. "Because I know better. And defensive, Derek, I'm not. Suspicious — yes. Very.

23

Why don't you get to the point? *What do you want?*"

"First," he replied firmly, "I want you to have a drink. It might have a dulling effect on that razor-edged tongue you're brandishing." He didn't wait for her assent, but clanged a bell on his desk, his eyes never leaving hers. "What would you like?"

She stood angrily and protested, "I do not want a drink! I want to finish this meeting and get out of here!"

She gasped with shock when all appearance of polite cordiality dropped from his features and he took one menacing step toward her, planting his hands on her shoulders and pushing her roughly back into the chair. "Sit, Mrs. Tremayne, and have a drink!" he ordered in a low growl. He did not release her, but continued to challenge her, his fingers biting into her flesh in subtle warning. "I insist."

The features above her were rigid and grim; the muscles that held her in their command were tense and strained. For a moment she stared into his angry brown eyes with indecision. She was no match for him on a physical level, but she could scream! Yet, what good would that do? She had the uneasy feeling that James would merely walk in stiffly with his usual calm, set a tray of drinks on the desk, ask Derek if there would be anything else, and totally ignore her whether she was screaming bloody murder or not!

"I'll take a glass of wine," she said glacially, refusing to blink as she met his commanding stare with marked resentment.

Derek moved away instantly. "Good, love. I'm glad to see that you're beginning to see things my way."

Leigh forgot her aloof reserve. "I'll never see things your way!" she cried, shocked by her own vehemence. Why was she allowing herself to become emotional?

Derek raised an arched brow in mock surprise. "What? Is that a crack I'm seeing in Madam Frost? How amazing! I thought that blood had long ago ceased to run in your veins!"

Leigh contained a retort as James chose that moment to enter the room. Derek requested a carafe of wine and as poker-faced as ever James exited to comply. As soon as the double doors were tightly closed, Leigh was once more on her feet, this time ready to do battle. A springing leap put the barrier of the chair between her and Derek.

"I'm getting out of here, Derek," she hissed with ringing bravado. "I was crazy to come. I knew all you wanted to do was insult me and —"

"Stop, please," Derek said quietly. He scratched his forehead tiredly and sighed. "I really didn't mean it to be like this. I'm sorry. It's just that you sailed in here like Her Majesty the Queen and I reacted badly. I knew this would be difficult for both of us. But maybe it's better that we started out this way. Maybe we've cleared the air a bit. Please, sit. We won't talk about the past or anything personal except in the context of the present. Agreed?"

Leigh watched Derek guardedly, feeling like a fox being conned by a hound. If only he had continued to be rude and harsh! Then she could have logically called a halt to their meeting and blamed the disaster on him!

She had to admit that she wanted to stay. When she had heard from Derek, after fourteen months of silence, she had been quite surprised. She told herself it was only curiosity that caused her to accept his invitation to Star Island for a "mutually beneficial" meeting. But although she would never admit it on a conscious level, it had not been curiosity that had brought her. Honestly not understanding why they *had* become bitter enemies, she still simply wanted to see him.

"All right, Derek," she said slowly, sidling back into the chair. "I'm willing to listen to what you've got to say."

This time he didn't hedge for a second. "I want to finish the rock opera on Henry the Eighth," he said bluntly.

She stared at him for several seconds without a muscle in her face moving. Then she whispered, "Why?"

"Because it is good."

Leigh looked down at her hands, dismayed to find that they were trembling. The rock opera was hers. Although Richard had often taken her work and ideas and claimed them as his, he had scoffed at the one composition she had put her most loving effort into. He told her it would never sell; he wanted nothing to do with it. To the best of her knowledge, Derek had only seen the rough draft once. He had displayed interest in the project, but that interest was quickly squelched by Richard, who had dismissed it with a wave of his hand, telling Derek with apparent loving humor that it was just an "exercise" for his wife. Leigh hadn't bothered to dispute him.

Now she glanced back to Derek, trying to find a motive for his renewed interest in his penetrating eyes. His expression told her nothing. Careful to keep her voice nonchalant, she reminded him, "You know that Richard didn't write any of the songs. He helped me with the music, but he didn't even like the work he did himself."

"I know."

Leigh crossed her legs and reached into her bag for a cigarette. Moving with surprising grace for a man his size, Derek took a marble lighter from his desk and was on his haunches in front of her to light a flame before she could. She wished she had never dived for the cigarette. It was hard enough to hide her pleasure over his apparent belief in her work with him several feet away; having him so close that she could feel his warm breath on her cheeks had made it an impossible task.

"I haven't looked at it since Richard died," she said noncommittally.

"I doubted that you had," Derek said without moving. His presence at her side, literally at her feet, was totally unnerving. She could smell a pleasant hint of musky cologne, feel the vigorous, coiled tension that made him so very alive and exciting.

Exhaling a long plume of smoke, avoiding his eyes, she asked quietly, "What did you have in mind?"

He raised teasing brows and she blushed. "I mean, do you want me to give you what I have? Are you going to take it from there? Are we going to bill it as Richard's final work? I'm not sure he'd like that."

Derek finally stood and ambled back to his desk, running his fingers through his curly hair. "No, no, no, and you're probably right. I want you to plan on staying here for the next month. You and I will finish it together. We won't bill it as Richard's work, although he will be listed in the credits."

A knock on the double doors prevented Leigh from making a stunned reply. James entered with the wine on a silver tray as she had expected. He deftly poured and delivered two glasses, nodded in response to their mumbled thank yous, and decorously left them, closing the doors with a definitive snap. Leigh took a long sip of wine and finally spoke, breaking the uncomfortable silence that had formed between them. "You are either crazy, a sadist, a masochist, or all three!" she breathed uneasily.

Derek broke into spontaneous laughter and hefted himself to a sitting position on his desk. "I can never say you aren't honest about your feelings!" He chuckled. He twirled his wineglass and absently watched the gold liquid as it rolled about. His voice tightened harshly as he added, "But don't worry. I know what they are. Still, we got along very well at one time. I think we could work together on a strictly professional basis."

"But, Derek!" Leigh protested. "I couldn't possibly stay *here!*"

"And why not?"

"Because . . . because . . ."

"Are you worried about your reputation?" he demanded scornfully.

"No . . ."

"Then what's the problem?"

"Oh, Derek!" she exclaimed with disgust. "You know perfectly well what the problem is! I have no intention of staying with or working with a man who considers me responsible for —" She choked, unable to go on.

"Don't!" he scoffed coldly. "Don't play the bereaved widow with me! I know all about the divorce papers! I know Richard asked you — for a reconciliation! I know you turned him down flat. So let's keep everything on an honest level. I think the work you were doing was good. I'm sure you'd like to see it become a reality. I can help you. We both make money, we possibly come out with a memorable piece of music. That's all."

Leigh wanted to scream. She wanted to shout the truth into Derek's callous face. Sure, Richard had never wanted the divorce. But he wanted their marriage to stay on *his terms*. And those terms meant that Richard did what and saw whom he wanted. Leigh stayed home, always there when he decided he needed her, quiet, loving, and unquestioning, even when Richard came in at four A.M. with lipstick stains on his shirts and musky odors of unfamiliar perfumes.

She didn't scream or shout. Rising slowly, she crushed out her cigarette and set her half-consumed glass of wine on the desk, ignoring Derek. She walked back to the chair and picked up her bag before turning to him. "Derek, I can't work with you. We don't seem to be able to carry on a simple conversation. You have your opinions . . . I can't seem to change them and I don't know if I care what you think anyway. Thanks for calling me, though, it was a nice thought."

She should have completed her explanation, spun on her heels, and walked right out the doors with her dignity intact. But

31

she didn't. She hesitated, just a second, but a second too long. Derek was at her side, cajoling her with a pointed challenge.

"Really, Leigh!" he admonished as he gently took her bag from her and tossed it back on the chair. "I never thought of you as the whiny, oversensitive kind. I do apologize — I did promise not to bring up the past. But madam! To run so quickly! If my memory isn't faulty, love, you do know how to put one in one's place. You aren't afraid of me, are you?"

"No!" Leigh exclaimed. She hoped her voice held conviction.

"Marvelous." Derek grinned wickedly and Leigh inwardly acknowledged and saluted his charisma and power of persuasion. It was easy to understand why nations of women, from teenyboppers to graying matrons, fell madly, if distantly, in love with him. He was the strength, the vision, the talent that had kept the group at the top of music charts for almost twenty years.

"Now," he continued, and she realized that he had subtly guided her to the highly polished grand piano. "Refresh my mind. Let me hear the opening song."

"I — I can't!" she faltered.

"Why not? I don't see any broken fingers

on your hands!" He pretended to test them for mobility as he manipulated her body onto the bench. "And don't tell me you haven't played since Richard's death!" he chastised her sternly. "I won't believe you!"

Leigh glanced nervously over her shoulder to find that he had taken a stance behind her, his hands in his pockets, his eyes riveted on the piano keys. "But I told you!" she hedged, "I haven't looked at 'Henry the Eighth' since . . . then." Moistening her lips, she tried to bring the blurring black and white keys into focus. She couldn't play! Not with Derek standing over her shoulder! The scene was too familiar. She trembled as it brought the sharp pain of memory. Leigh, sitting at the piano, aglow with excitement and the desire to please, Richard changing that excitement to misery with harsh and amused showers of ridicule . . .

"Leigh . . ." It was amazing how soft and gentle Derek's voice could be at times. "The piece is good. So okay, you'll be rusty. You haven't played it in a while. This isn't a royal performance. I just want to get the taste in my mouth."

Three of Leigh's delicate, manicured fingers touched lightly on ivory, but the freezing chill of fear that assaulted her was too strong. If she stayed at the keyboard any longer, her hands would fly to her face and she would dissolve into a mass of sobbing shudders. And dear Lord! That was something she could never do in front of Derek! He wouldn't understand, and he'd rip her apart.

Holding her head high, she slid with feigned indifference from the stool. "Sorry, Derek," she said coolly. "It's no good. I just don't remember any of it." She stooped nonchalantly for her bag and glided regally for the door. "But like I said, thanks for the thought!"

She was surprised when Derek made no attempt to stop her departure. Pausing at the door to wave a crisp good-bye, she found that he had taken her position at the piano and was softly playing the chords of one of the group's top hits — a mellow love ballad he had written fifteen years ago but which could still be heard frequently on a multitude of radio stations.

"Bye, Leigh," he said without glancing up. "Sorry I had you take the long drive for nothing. Keep in touch."

A large knot seemed to restrict her throat. Derek had started to sing the words in his husky tenor, a voice that had undoubtedly helped in many a seduction throughout the world. It sent a sharp stab of yearning through her even as she realized that what she listened to was just a well-written song performed by a gifted singer. Hell! she thought miserably. The haunting power of music was unfair.

"Good-bye, Derek," she called, marching out the doors and closing them tightly behind her. She started down the tiled hallway, still hearing the dimmed, but nevertheless compelling, sound of his voice. She clicked her heels loudly, yet even that didn't help. By the time she reached the outer doorway, she had come face to face with a terrible truth.

She, just like a million other heartsick "groupies," was in love with Derek Mallory. She had been, for quite some time. Only self-defense had allowed her the illusion that she had used him.

Oh, Lord! she prayed silently as she continued down the steps to her car. Please, just let me get out of here before I do something stupid in front of this electronic eye!

Although she was walking normally, her mind was racing with tormented confusion. How could she be such a fool as to be in love with Derek? Even if he cared two cents for her, *he was just like Richard.* Another musician, another *star.* One in a lifetime was burden enough for any one human to bear. Besides, she rationalized as she reached the haven of her car, she couldn't really be in love with Derek. She hadn't seen him until today in half a year. And sane people didn't fall in love with people who considered them to be cold, cruel, conniving, and mercenary!

She tilted the brim of her hat and slid her key into the ignition. It would be all right; in just a matter of minutes she would be across the Island bridge and she would probably never see him again. She would get over her absurd fancy and continue with her life as usual, calm now, uncomplicated and complacent.

At first she thought the car's refusal to start was a figment of her wildly rushing imagination. Perhaps she hadn't really turned the key yet. But as she twisted it a second time to no avail, she was forced to accept the fact that for some reason the Audi had gone stone-cold dead. She sat dazed for a moment, incredulous that such a thing could be happening. She had had her mechanic check beneath the hood and fill the car with gas only that morning, just an hour before she had left her Key West home to travel the few hours north to Miami. Furiously, she turned the key a third, fourth, and fifth time, but the Audi refused to choke out a single sound.

Derek! The man would stoop to anything to get his own way. Her recent self-admittance of her emotions regarding him added fuel to the fire of her wrath. Steaming to a point of explosion, she scrambled from the car, viciously slammed the door, and stormed back into the house, brushing past James imperiously and striding down the hall toward Derek's office with long, angry steps. She burst in on him like a tornado, seething so hotly that she not only forgot her aloofness entirely, but found it difficult not to rush straight for his neck and attempt to throttle him.

"What did you do to my car?" she raged.

Derek glanced at her disdainfully from the piano bench, twisting his wiry frame to observe better her irate, quivering form. "I didn't do a damn thing to your car," he said coldly.

"Then why won't it start?" Leigh challenged.

"How the hell would I know!" he exclaimed impatiently. "I'm not omniscient!" His eyes roamed with indifferent amusement from the brim of her hat to her crisp beige heels, then he turned back to the keyboard with a shrug. "Buzz James. He'll get someone to look at it for you."

Leigh's pent-up emotions erupted. With a shrill curse she sent her bag flying across the room, hurtling it with such venomous force and an uncannily correct aim that it struck Derek smartly in the back of his leonine head. Leigh gasped with shock, horrified by her own behavior, and was immediately filled with remorse. Her anger drained from her as she watched Derek slowly turn again, rising to his full, imposing height, and move swiftly toward her, his eyes narrowed and glittering with glacial fury. She opened her mouth to apologize, but no sound came. The possible repercussions of her hostile act were dawning on her with rapid clarity. Derek, when pushed to anger, showed little mercy. She knew he often restrained his emotions because, once let loose, his temper could be a terrible thing, savage and wild.

It had only been seconds since Leigh had struck him with her flying missile, but time seemed frozen as he approached her. Thoughts whirled through her mind with the speed of light. It was too bad he didn't seem to have a sense of humor at the moment. It was almost funny. She usually couldn't hit the side of a barn with a tennis ball!

Her stunned immobility came to an end when Derek was almost upon her. A flash of logical panic came to her and she decided to make a hasty retreat. She had only seen him really angry once, but she knew she didn't want to see him so again — especially if she were to be the object of that anger. Spinning with the true speed of acute fear, she scurried for the doors and escape.

Her effort came too late. Even as she turned, her hat went flying from her head, and her attempt to flee was painfully curtailed as Derek's forceful fingers gripped into the neat knot of auburn hair, sending the pins cascading to the floor, wrenching her into an abrupt aboutface. She cried out; her liquid eyes and trembling lips begged silently for forgiveness. But Derek was not yet ready to show compassion. His fingers remained tightly clenched in the now tumbled, soft disarray of her hair, pulling her head back so that her neck arched cruelly and she had no choice but to meet his stern, unrelenting features, stare into his smoldering golden-brown eyes. His other hand, she noted vaguely, had fallen to her waist, pressing her dangerously close to his lean hips and powerfully muscled thighs. She could feel his breath on her cheeks, see a row of clenched, straight white teeth, sense the tickle of his soft beard on her flesh. For a brief moment she wondered if he were going to strike her or kiss her. . . .

He did neither. A struggle for control played across his features, then he released her and walked tersely to his desk, leaned against it, and rang the buzzer. Scrutinizing her with quiet contempt, he advised, "You might want to brush your hair. James will be here in a second."

Shaking with humiliation, Leigh scurried across the room for her bag, extracted her brush, and tried to put some order into the long, thick tresses, which hung over her face and down her back in gold-hued, fluffy tangles. She had just completed her task when James entered the room, but if he noticed that their guest had lost her hat and sophisticated upsweep, he gave no sign. Derek explained that Mrs. Tremayne was having auto difficulty and would James please see to it. The butler nodded and started to leave but Derek halted him with, "Oh, and, James, will you ask Emma to prepare a guest room and tell her that Mrs. Tremayne will be staying for dinner?

Thank you." The oak doors were closed again.

Leigh shot Derek a hostile glance and stated firmly, "Mrs. Tremayne will not be staying the night!"

"Then Mrs. Tremayne is a bigger fool than I thought," Derek said smoothly. "Don't you ever read weather reports or listen to the radio?"

Leigh's hostility changed to confusion. "I — I don't know what you're talking about!"

"The tropical storm over Cuba has increased to hurricane velocity," Derek said, idly searching the cobalt shag of his office carpeting for her hairpins. "You would have been all right if you could have left now, but, say, five or six hours from now the outer winds will be hitting the Keys. Unless it takes a radical change of course."

"Oh." Leigh stood awkwardly. She was a fool! She had heard something about a tropical storm brewing in the Caribbean. Why hadn't she paid more attention to the reports? She should have never left her home to begin with! As a native "Conch," or Key Westerner, she had seen many a storm thunder its ferocity upon the island. Her home, she felt, was safe. Knowing her

41

native habitat as she did, she had insisted that Richard have it built to exacting specifications. Usually when storm warnings threatened, she stocked the house well, filled every receptacle in it with water, and offered it as a harbor to others in less fortunate positions — those who were not able to evacuate or felt their own homes were dangerous during the deluge of water and wrecking winds.

But in the last few days she had been terribly absentminded. All she had thought about was her approaching appointment with Derek. She had not picked up a newspaper, barely glanced at the TV, and, if she had heard a radio, she didn't remember a thing said.

And now here she was, virtually a prisoner of the feckless gods of fate, stuck with Derek due to the haphazard whimsy of the weather. "I'm sure there can't be anything seriously wrong with my car," she said in a small voice tinged with hope as she absently reknotted her hair.

Derek, holding his cache of pins, advanced on her nonchalantly. "Don't," he said curtly, pushing her hands from her hair. "It looks much nicer down. I never did like the way Richard tried to dress you up like a porcelain doll." He handed her the pins and strode with assurance toward the doors. "Excuse me, I need to shower and change for dinner."

"But, Derek . . ." Leigh's protest trailed away.

"Yes?"

"I — I can't stay! I have nothing with me!"

He hesitated slightly, one powerful hand curling around the edge of a door. A small, humorously tender smile showed beneath the trimmed hair of his beard. "I remember you used to wear Richard's tailored shirts to bed." His grin broadened across his face. "I have a zillion shirts. Take your pick. And Emma's always prepared for anything. She keeps a horde of soap, toothpaste, shampoo, and the like that would make a drugstore look understocked. She'll take care of you."

The door began to close but Leigh once more felt compelled to stop her host, deciding the temperance of his behavior after her own childish display warranted an apology. "Derek!" she called again stiffly, not quite able to sound truly humble. "I'm sorry."

"Are you? How nice." The friendly grin had left his face and the eyes that bored into her were unfathomable. He seemed distracted for a moment, then added in a low tone with a rough edge that could only be deciphered as a warning, "But you should learn to guard that temper of yours. Richard might have tolerated it — he had to, you were his wife. But I rarely make allowances more than once."

"Well how good of you to leave me unscathed this once!" Leigh drawled sarcastically. Although she knew better, she couldn't seem to stop herself from goading him. "If —" she stated with pronounced accusation, "if my car hadn't gone mysteriously dead, it never would have happened!"

"My dear Mrs. Tremayne," he said, shaking his head slightly as if he had been delegated the task of explaining something to a very small child. A scornful smile twisted his handsome features. "Dear, dear woman! Do you really imagine I would ever have to stoop to trickery to keep a lady in the house if I so desired?"

A scarlet blush rose unbidden to her cheeks. Tossing her hair behind her shoulders, she attempted a comeback to dispel the miserable feeling of utter ridiculousness he had instilled in her. "My dear Mr. Mallory! Believe it or not, there are women in the world who value the trait of modesty. You never know, one of them might be more than willing to turn you down!"

"True, love, but the sea is full of fish."

"And one black cat is just like another in the dark?"

"You got it."

Leigh gave him a saccharin-sweet smile. "That's what you think now, Derek Mallory. But one day you'll change your tune. You are a mere mortal — or were you aware of that? One day, Mr. Music, you will fall in love. And I hope you're on your knees begging for the feeling to be reciprocated, begging for marriage —"

"Oh doubtful, love! Doubtful!" Derek interrupted casually. "You see, I saw a friend fall in love, and I saw what it did to him. The beautiful, shy little creature that he married turned out to be a heartless bitch. No, I don't foresee the same thing happening to me."

He had barely gotten the words out of his mouth before Leigh was on him, hand raised, nails curved like a feline's in a hissing attack. Once again she hadn't bothered to think about her actions. She had forgotten all about any of her gentler emotions toward Derek; all she knew was that at that moment she hated him with black and thorough rage.

Her blow never found its mark. He must have anticipated that his provoking remark would draw such a response from her. Catching her hand with deft ease, he twisted it cruelly behind her back. "Oh, Leigh!" he said, his voice dripping disgust. "You never do learn, do you? I'm not your doting, besotted husband. Don't ever slap me, I slap back." His jaw tightened savagely. "And believe me, woman, if ever a man lived who thought you deserved a sound thrashing, that man is me. So don't tempt me, huh? I'd love to give you a good taste of your just reward!"

Leigh was in no position to argue. The pain in her steel-trapped arm was barely endurable. But she wouldn't apologize. Not ever again! He was so — so wrong and unfair! Despite the agony she felt, she tilted her head in defiance and stared at him distastefully. "I loathe you, Mr. Mallory," she said, the green overshadowing the amber in her eyes, gleaming emerald with open vehemence. "You are the most arrogant, egotistical, self-righteous, self-centered bas—" she stopped as a cry of agony escaped her lips as Derek twisted her arm even more viciously. She closed her eyes miserably and fell silent. With a slight push, he released her.

"Sorry, I can't stand here and listen to any more of your opinions," he said as if they had been discussing a song or a book. "I don't want to be late for dinner. I have a guest coming later this evening and I want you tucked in for the night before she arrives. I won't need any of your opinions with her here, either."

He saluted her quickly and headed for the curving staircase that ranged to the right of his office and the hallway. As soon as he moved, Leigh forced her quivering and abused limbs quickly to retrieve her bag for a final time and to rush back down the hallway in a desperate dash for the door. Hurricane or no, she wasn't staying here! She'd happily walk the distance back to the mainland and stand on the causeway until someone picked her up and got her to a phone; she'd do anything to get away from Derek.

"I wouldn't do that if I were you!" his voice suddenly warned as she set her hands on the outer door. "The dogs are out. Nice nasty Dobermans. They chew strangers into little bits!"

Leigh clenched her teeth as she let her hand fall from the door. "Then call me a cab, please."

"Sorry, love." Derek's mock apology

echoed frostily against the tile. "Phones are dead. We've been having that problem frequently this past month. Cable trouble."

The echo died slowly as he continued up the stairway. "Damn you!" Leigh cried, shaking with misery and despair. "Damn you, Derek! Why did you make me come here?"

But he was gone. He didn't hear her, nor did he see the abject tears that shimmered on her eyelashes and fell to her cheeks, or the frightened unhappiness that trembled on her lips.

Chapter Two

The view from the arched balcony off the guest bedroom Leigh had been allotted was stunning. Before her lay the shimmering rectangular pool and beyond it the deep blue water of the channel separating Star Island from the causeway. If she cast her eyes to the left, she could see the high rises of Miami Beach, twinkling now in the dusk like a million merry stars. To the right, in a distant glimmer of reflection, was Biscayne Bay, choppy with the fringe of winds caused by the tropical storm southward. Each foam-flecked wave danced and gleamed like a diamond, caught in the nighttime brilliance of the *Miami Herald* building and the magnificent OMNI complex beyond it.

Graceful steps led from the balcony to the palm-fringed pool, and Leigh was sorely tempted to follow them down and touch the silver enchantment of the water. With a regretful shake of her head she decided against such action. She had already been standing on the balcony, hyp-

notized by the display of the various surrounding waters, for a good half hour.
Derek's housekeeper had supplied her with
an assortment of toiletries, and she wanted
to shower before dinner even if she did
have to redon the same clothing.

The huge, inviting deco tub in the bathroom, along with the enticing bottle of
bath oil that had been supplied her, was
too much of a temptation to allow her to
settle for a simple shower. She filled the
claw-footed tub with deliciously hot water,
added the oil; then, after carefully hanging
her clothes, she sank her tense limbs into
the luxurious, misting heat.

It was a pity, Leigh thought, closing her
eyes in total surrender to the comfort, that
she, considered to be such a cool bastion
of reserve, didn't seem to be able to maintain an ounce of casual dignity where
Derek was concerned. Why on earth had
she allowed herself to behave so badly?
Wanting Derek's respect so very much, it
seemed she was only capable of drawing
his contempt.

Well, the hell with it! she decided, suddenly angry. He had judged her without a
trial, formed an opinion without half the
facts. He was a devastatingly attractive
man, but she had met many an attractive

man. And Leigh was a strong realist. Life always went on. She would get away as soon as possible.

A knock on the door interrupted her mental wanderings as she was rising from the tub and rubbing her skin to a rough gleam with a large navy towel. She didn't have time to call out; Derek's cheery housekeeper had tucked her head into the bedroom and was calling out, "Just me, Mrs. Tremayne. May I come in?"

Leigh wrapped the towel tightly around herself and peeked out from the bathroom. "Sure, Emma. But you'll have to pardon my dress!"

Emma Larson was a plump little lady, and although she preferred to stay in the background, she ruled Derek's house with a firm hand, from the domestic employees to Derek himself. Even dignified James bowed before her. The toughest elements of the music industry who paid calls upon Derek behaved like lambs in Emma's presence. With her shrewd, crisp blue eyes, she brought them all down to size, seeing clearly through all their facades. Leigh wondered briefly and with a touch of fear whether or not Emma might also see all too clearly through her. Then she smiled as she exited the bath in her towel. If Emma did come uncomfortably close to reading her mind, she would contain her thoughts. Though they had met only once before, two years ago when Leigh and Richard had come for a week to work out a concert schedule, Leigh and Emma had become friends by some unspoken agreement. Though Emma had always been polite and proper toward Richard, Leigh had the uncanny feeling that Emma was unimpressed by his charm or his person and had secretly pitied Leigh even then.

"Wonderful, sweetie!" Emma proclaimed as she bustled into the room and deposited a couple of boxes on the room's elegant four-poster bed. "I'm glad I caught you before you had time to dress. Derek sent one of the boys over to town to pick up a few things for you."

Leigh stared at the boxes dumbly for a few seconds. "You mean . . ." she said hesitantly, half stunned, half angry, "you mean Derek sent someone out to buy clothing for me?"

"Oh, no, darling!" Emma said with horror. "Derek called the shop himself. All the boy did was pick them up!" She gave Leigh a friendly wink. "Derek claims he knows your taste and your size. He ordered from the same place where he's often purchased your birthday and Christmas gifts!" Emma smiled brightly and turned her little figure for the door. "I'll leave you now, unless I can do something else. Dinner will be about thirty minutes."

"I'm fine, Emma, thank you," Leigh said. It would be fruitless to tell the housekeeper she didn't want anything from Derek Mallory — especially clothing!

She dressed quickly in her own suit, ignoring the boxes. She would inform Derek that she couldn't accept such gifts from him. After brushing and rearranging her hair and freshening her makeup, she walked determinedly to the door. But her determination did not quite make it. Curiosity called her back into the room.

The first box contained a pair of designer jeans and a handsome western shirt. An outfit for the following day she assumed. Pursing her lips, she closed the box. Opening the second, she let out a shocked gasp. A beautiful, simple beige cocktail dress of angel-fine silk met her eyes. Being female, she couldn't help but draw it from the box and against her form to whirl before the mirror.

The dress, of sleek lines, was made to form sensuously around the body. It was, as Derek had boasted, perfect to her taste and size. She itched to step into it, but though her fingers lovingly caressed the material, she forced herself to fold it carefully and to return it to the box. Repacking the gown, she realized that there was more in the box. A blush rose to her cheeks as she discovered stockings, a slip, bikini underwear, and a lacy, lowcut bra — all also perfectly sized.

Good Lord! she thought, quivering. How could he know her measurements so exactly? Her presents from him over the years had often been clothing, but never such intimate apparel! But then, she thought, with a wry and rueful twist of anger, Derek was a connoisseur of women. He could probably take any female figure and size it up easily. With that in mind she quickly closed the box and marched stiffly from the room.

"Mr. Mallory is on the patio, Mrs. Tremayne," James informed her as she reached the landing. "May I bring you a cocktail?"

Leigh was about to refuse, then she decided a drink might be in order. The right amount of liquor might sharpen her tongue rather than dull it, and she would need a bit of a bite to get through the evening. "Thank you, James," she said. "A vodka and tonic would be nice."

The butler nodded and Leigh braced herself mentally and physically as she made her way through the parlor with its simple yet elegant period furnishings and strode with no visible trace of hesitancy to the poolside.

Derek was standing at the far end, facing the channel. He cradled a glass absently in both hands as his tawny eyes fastened on the blue night before him. He was dressed now in a brown velvet three-piece suit, and Leigh was struck afresh by his aura of power and charisma. The suit, which should have covered his tapered physique, enhanced it. He turned to her then, and as a frown furrowed into his features, she was hit with another, startling realization. He had shaved off his beard!

Surprise was about to make her comment on the disturbing fact but Derek spoke before she could. "Why are you wearing that?" he demanded flatly.

"Because," Leigh replied equally blandly, "though I do appreciate the thought, Derek, I do not care to accept such gifts from you. You needn't have gone to the bother. But I haven't touched the things. You can return them tomorrow." Color was spreading through her face despite the unconcerned tone of her voice. She was remembering the intimate "gifts" and the precision of their order. The wind whipped at the escaping tendrils of her hair and she turned toward the channel with carefully planned nonchalance. "Your turn!" she challenged jauntily. "What happened to your beard?"

Derek lightly rubbed the fresh and tender skin of his squared jawline. "Down the drain, love. And all for your benefit. I remember you saying you hated scratchy beards!" He moved to her and ran a finger along her cheek. "So you see" — his touch was like a whisper of air and his voice as soft — "I'm willing to accommodate you to drastic lengths. I think you could humor me in return and wear the dress."

Those tawny eyes were boring into hers and she didn't seem able to turn away. She felt like a deer trapped in the headlights of an approaching car, hypnotized and searching in spite of the coming danger. But she had to move. She was quite sure that Derek was about to take her into his arms, an easy conquest like his other "interchangeable" cats, and she had to avoid such a catastrophe at all costs. He moved even closer, and she found the strength to force her own unwilling limbs.

She took a giant step backward, and tumbled straight into the pool.

Derek's laughter reached her ears even through the insulation of the chlorinated water. Furious from the sound, she refused to surface, but swam the depths to the shallow end instead and climbed up the circular steps, high heels in her hands.

"Looks like you'll have to change after all," he commented evenly.

Leigh didn't reply. She marched for the house, just in time to run into James and her vodka and tonic. "Thank you, James," she said airily, sweeping the glass from the small silver tray. "I'll bring this up with me." She sailed on past him, as cool as he despite the rivulets of water that drained from her. Once inside and out of vision, she pelted up the steps quickly, wondering if James would smirk along with Derek behind her back. Besides, she was freezing. The water had been warm, but the stiff wind had chilled her to the bone.

In the privacy of her room she stripped off her soaking clothing and stepped into a quick shower to rinse the chill and the smell of the chemicals from her skin. Then she donned the new clothing bitterly, noting that Derek couldn't have manipulated her into submission any better had he planned it. Or had he planned it?

What was he up to? she asked herself as she pinned her sodden hair. It wasn't a romantic interlude; he had already told her he was expecting a date later and he wanted her out of the way. Besides, he disliked and distrusted her! She knew his displays of courtesy were often masks. No, he was up to something. She didn't believe for one minute that his sole reason for summoning her had been the music. He could write circles around her any day of the week. Then what? Revenge? Punishment for what she had supposedly done to Richard? How absurd. There wasn't really anything he could do to her.

Or was there? She was already stuck where she didn't want to be in the home of a man she had once sworn never to see again.

She tilted her chin proudly and smiled a brave smile to the woman in the mirror. That was much better. The lost and frightened look was gone. Of course she didn't have to go down to dinner. She could hide up here and simply disappear in the morning without seeing Derek. Yes, she could run away.

No. The smile she gave herself was stronger and more sincere. She was not a gawking, naive teen-ager. She had been the wife of Richard Tremayne; she had learned to hold her own and survive in a rugged world. She would tuck tail and run before no one — not even Derek Mallory! And if he wanted to play games, well, she could play them too. She had proved that once. It was a pity that Derek would never know how well she played a game.

It was a greater pity that she had paid so dearly for that game — paid with dreams, longing, yearning, physical pain.

The sick, agonized look was returning to her eyes. She left the room, pushing the memory to the back of her mind as she usually managed to do. Usually, in rational thought, she pretended that the night had been a dream. The man, the chivalrous King Arthur, had not been Derek, just as she had not been the exotic belly dancer. It had all been a fantasy, not real. As far as she was concerned, she *hadn't* seen Derek since Richard's funeral; she hadn't even attended the party in Atlanta.

And if she was in love, *it was with a fantasy*, not Derek Mallory.

The attractive male who had been dominating her mind greeted her with a long, low wolf whistle. She had to laugh. Derek, minus the beard, seemed younger tonight, more gallant, more touchable. Had he really razored off his magnificent beard on her behalf? Maybe. But, she reminded herself primly, it would be a grave mistake to lower her guard, no matter what his guise might be. She dug her nails into the palm of her hand. They knew exactly who one another was this night. They could never in reality escape the past or the words that had passed between them.

"Thank you," she said demurely, in full control. She spun a graceful pirouette to allow the folds of the dress to swirl smoothly around her. "You do have a nice eye for clothing, Mr. Mallory."

Derek nodded gravely in acceptance of her compliment, but she noticed that his eyes held a satanish twinkle as he answered, "I have an eye for what would become certain spectacular forms."

"Thank you again," Leigh said casually. "I hope I haven't delayed dinner. I want to be certain to 'disappear' before your date arrives." She astonished herself with the total lack of concern in her statement.

"Umm . . ." Derek was noncommittal. "I'll be sure to have you well out of the way when she arrives." He wore a pleasant grin as he approached her and offered his arm. "Shall we go in to dinner? James said to come in as soon as you were ready."

Dinner was served in the small nook off the kitchen. Prepared for two, the meal was as elegant as any planned for the most romantic honeymoon. James poured champagne into glittering crystal glasses; candles flickered a mellow glow over the slender centerpiece of red and yellow roses. The main course was stone crabs, a Florida delicacy they both favored. For the first portion of the meal they concentrated on the food and kept the conversation light and bantering. But it was inevitable that trouble spring up, despite the pains taken by James and Emma to create a soothing atmosphere.

It started innocently enough. They had been discussing water levels in Key West when Derek suddenly leaned back, a half smile on his unusually bare features. "You know," he said, idly rubbing a long finger along the ridge of his champagne glass, "I'll never forget the day Richard and I met you. You looked like a little waif coming from the ocean, like the mermaid who sold her soul for human legs." He laughed ruefully. "We were both out to impress you — until we discovered you could outswim us in a matter of seconds! I think Richard fell in love with you the moment you dove out of his reach."

Leigh felt a piece of the tender crab catch in her throat. "Richard always did want what he couldn't reach," she said softly when she could.

If she had meant to keep the peace, she should have kept her mouth shut. But her reply had been nothing less than the truth. Still, she knew as she watched Derek's jawline harden and his gold eyes glimmer as if they were about to light like the fire of the candle before them that he had construed her comment as further criticism of her dead husband. His next words verified her apprehension.

"We were both captivated by you, Mrs. Tremayne," he said coldly. "I, like Richard, believed you to be refreshingly guileless and innocent. I even believed you had no idea who we were."

"I didn't know who you were!" Leigh exclaimed indignantly. "I had heard of the London Company, of course; your first album came out when I was in third grade! But how on earth would I have recognized you? I'd never been to a concert! And you always wore some sort of costume on your album covers! And anyway, *Mr. Mallory*, I might remind you that not everyone is impressed by members of the music world!"

"Possibly," Derek acknowledged. "But most people are impressed by money."

Leigh inhaled sharply and tossed her napkin on the table before rising. "I never wanted Richard's money!" she declared hotly. "Nor his 'impressive' name nor 'impressive' companions! If you care to do some research into my finances, you'll find I've not run wild on anything of his! I live in a home which I helped finance and create, I give large sums to the children's care centers and —"

"Richard wanted a child of his own," Derek interrupted rudely.

"Then he should have stayed home to have one!" Leigh retorted. "Excuse me," she added with regal cool. "This conversation has gone far enough. I don't care to discuss my personal life with Richard with anyone, especially you." She was dangerously close to tears. "Thank you for the gown, thank you for dinner and your hospitality. If my car is ready, I'll probably be gone before you rise. Good luck with whatever."

"Leigh!" Derek's commanding voice stopped her as she reached the door. She turned back to him expressionlessly.

"Where were you when Richard died?"

"I was at home, in Key West. Richard, as

you know, was on the West Coast. I hadn't seen him in two months. You must have known that too."

"No, I didn't," Derek said softly.

She didn't quite understand the agony that bared for a brief moment in his eyes. "It doesn't really make any difference."

"No, it doesn't."

For a reason she couldn't define, Leigh hesitated. "Derek?"

"Yes?"

"Do you know exactly what happened?"

"He went off a cliff."

"I know . . . but . . ."

"Cut and dried. No drugs involved. He probably had a few drinks, but he wasn't stoned, if that's what you're referring to." Derek dropped his own napkin on the mahogany table and walked to join her at the door. He very lightly cupped her chin in his hands, and she could feel a tingle that seemed to shoot straight through her as his fingers brushed her temples. For a moment, as his eyes searched hers in an unaccustomed tenderness, the months rolled away and she was frighteningly reminded of that one long-ago night. With painful recall she remembered the feel of his strong arms, the taste of his lips, the wonderful harmony of his sinewed body with hers. With precision she knew the touch of his skin, the shape of his magnificent form, the perfection of his lovemaking. . . .

"Derek, please," she murmured weakly. "I have a terrible headache. I need to get to sleep and your date . . ."

He kissed her, silencing her effectively. She stiffened at first and attempted to push away from him. But she was caught between the wall and his steellike strength; her attempt to budge him was futile and then feeble. His lips, like his eyes, were magnetic. They claimed hers with a firm tenderness, neither forcing nor allowing for escape. And as her resistance failed her, his tongue feathered along her teeth until it probed and found access to her warm, sweet moistness, to demand in earnest. That which had been gentle became passionate and demanding, urgent and hungry. The warnings in Leigh's mind went unheeded as her flesh burned from the arousing possession of his subtly exploring hands. They traced the graceful angle of her neck, warmed her back and shoulders to a glow of anticipation, hovered over her breasts until a hot chill of desire blotted out everything except . . .

The shrill cry of the door bell.

Sanity returned. Leigh stared at Derek with horror, watched as triumphant amusement crept into his eyes, then fled from the doorway and up the staircase just as James was opening the door. Reaching the sanctuary of solitude, she dimly heard the musical tinkle of a female voice as she closed her own bedroom door and bolted it firmly. She was shaking from head to toe, consumed by hot and cold, shamed, humiliated, and . . . empty.

She stared at the bolted door for a while, then began mechanically to pull the pins from her still-damp hair. Glancing over at the bed, she began to tremble anew as she saw an assortment of tailored shirts. Some were short-sleeved, some long-sleeved. They were Derek's. He hadn't forgotten his offer.

Her first instinct was to push the lot of them onto the floor. But that action would be foolish. Emma would be the one to suffer. She watched them warily instead, as if they might come alive and attack her. Then she sighed, kicked off her shoes, and disrobed. She chose a long-sleeved pin-stripe with tails that reached halfway to her knees and began to pace the room as she buttoned it. She was coming down with a ferocious headache. Perhaps the night air could help clear the tension causing the pain. Barefoot and clad only in the absurdly large shirt, she opened the sliding doors to the balcony and stepped out into the wind. She slid the door closed behind her and leaned against it as the salt breeze tickled her face. It did feel good. The house was air-conditioned and comfortable, but there was nothing like the air of the sea on a night such as this.

She stood for a long time, thinking. She would never forget the day that she had met Richard and Derek either. She had been idly snorkling in the surf off her father's beach house when she had risen from the water to discover the two handsome young men wandering along, apparently lost. She had informed them that they were on private property, but they had quickly cajoled her into entertaining them. Their names — first ones only were given — didn't mean a thing to her. She knew of the London Company — everyone did. They had cut their first gold album when all were still in their teens. Their work in the first years came out sporadically as each spent time in acclaimed music schools. Then, as graduates, they began to put out a constant flow of quality work. Before the oldest member, Richard, reached thirty, all five members were millionaires and celebrities. They had scored movies and plays, appeared on prestigious television specials, and performed before president and queen.

But when Leigh came across Richard and Derek, she accepted them as a pair of poor, confused British tourists. They had talked awhile, flirted in the gently rolling waves, and then Leigh had invited them for dinner. Her dad had been alive then, and the occasion had been tremendous, her father showing a definite interest in Derek. Both men had courted her teasingly, but Derek had been involved with a buxomy stewardess at the time and it was Richard who pursued her, a little awed at the discovery of his fame, to the altar. Richard wanted a wife. A wife, she discovered, to be a centerpiece. But he was, at times, good to her. He had been her buffer from pain at her father's death; he had chosen Key West as his permanent home because she loved it. For certain kindnesses, she loved him.

And yet, she thought guiltily, she had never felt for Richard what she did for Derek. Her blood had never boiled at the near sight of him, she had never reached the plain of heaven in his arms. . . .

No! Although she didn't scream aloud, the word reverberated in her mind. She clenched her teeth and shivered, miserably regretting the folly of her masquerade with Derek. The night air didn't seem to be helping at all. She would be better off getting back into her room, calling downstairs and requesting a good stiff drink and a couple of aspirins.

She turned to do just that, but the glass wouldn't slide. She tried again, then considered the possibility of literally kicking herself. How could she have been so foolish? Only an idiot could lock herself out!

And she was locked out. She looked at the glass angrily and realized it must lock automatically when closed. Damn!

She pounded on the glass and yelled, but quickly ascertained the futility of such action. No one could hear her. She had only one choice, and that was to follow the stairs down to the patio and pool and re-enter the house on the ground floor. If she was lucky, she would avoid Derek and his date and only encounter Emma or James.

She took a deep breath and rushed down the stairs. If she had to run into someone, she might as well get it over with. She would certainly get nowhere fast by standing on the balcony shivering, her arms clasped tightly around herself.

The pool raced in silent ripples from the ever-increasing wind as she reached the empty patio, the palms bent low with each approaching salt-riddled gust. Leigh's hair whipped about her face in furious dishevelment as she hurried to the house, only to stop with abrupt confusion as she heard Derek's voice come clearly to her.

He was entertaining his guest in the rear salon. If she entered here, she would have to walk past them both and surely offer an explanation. "Damnation!" she muttered aloud. If there was anything she didn't want to do, it was to run into one of Derek's girl friends! And what would his girl friend think of a half-clad woman running about his house?

Cursing beneath her breath, Leigh decided to skirt around to the front of the house. Either James or Emma would answer the door — the front door was always kept locked — and meeting one of the household staff was definitely preferable.

She had not rounded the first corner before she heard the sound of vicious barking. Derek had not lied. The dogs were out. And she knew for a fact that they were Dobermans, mean and nasty unless they knew you and knew you belonged.

She did not belong. There was no time to lose. She ran like she had never run before in her life, back to the patio, straight into the salon. She slammed the door behind her, heart beating like a hunted rabbit's, beads of perspiration breaking out on her forehead. She had made it with just a few feet to spare. Two of the magnificent black creatures had been on her heels. They were now jumping on the door and howling their wrath.

The great gasps of her breathing began to subside, and she swept a stream of tangled auburn hair from her face and focused with dread on the room. Derek was standing; apparently he had been about to check on the cause of the frenzied animals. She expected he would be angry. Her presence in such attire could do little to enhance the romanticism of his date.

But he wasn't angry at all. If anything, his eyes were light and amused. She glanced apprehensively at his date. She wasn't a bit like Leigh would have imagined either. She was a woman of at least thirty-five or forty, attractive, but extremely businesslike and staid. Her rounded features bothered Leigh; she was sure she had seen the woman before.

"Really, Leigh!" Derek admonished in a lazy drawl. "If you wanted to join us, you could have simply dressed and come down the staircase."

Leigh shot him a look of pure hostility, but he seemed not to notice. Turning to the woman on the couch, he said, "Miss White, I believe you've met Leigh Tremayne before." He glanced back to Leigh. "Leigh, you must remember Lavinia White. She interviewed Richard several years ago for her magazine."

If there had been a hole in the floor anywhere, Leigh would have found it and crawled into it. This was ten times worse than breaking up the most passionate of romantic interludes. Derek's words reminded her immediately of where she had seen the woman before. Lavinia White. The queen of gossip columnists. Untouchable because she made sure all her articles were based on researched fact.

There was no hole in the floor to crawl into. Leigh winced with every nerve in her body, then forced herself to move away from the door. "Hello, Miss White," she said, sailing toward the woman and offering her hand as if she were dressed in heels and the most becoming of hostess gowns. "How are you?" Not waiting for a reply, she went on gaily to them both, "Please do excuse me. I'm afraid I locked myself out on the balcony. Terribly foolish, I know. Forgive me for the interruption."

"Oh, not at all, dear!" Lavinia White was smiling as smugly as the cat that had just caught the canary. Her twinkling green eyes told Leigh plainly that she was already planning the words of type to describe the state of dress in which she had found Leigh Tremayne in Derek Mallory's household. "In fact, I would have never forgiven Derek if you hadn't made an appearance. Why the rogue! He didn't even tell me you were here."

"Excuse me, ladies, if you will," Derek interrupted. "I want to see to the dogs." He grinned wickedly at Leigh before he exited and she knew exactly what he was thinking: You got yourself into this — now get yourself out of it!

Despite the sinking sensation in her heart, she smiled at Lavinia brightly. "Derek and I had some business to discuss this afternoon," she explained calmly, "then something went in my car. My home is in Key West, you know, and Derek didn't think it safe for me to drive back late with the storm so close and all . . ."

She had run out of her words of excuse and they were ringing false to her own ears anyway. She was in Derek's shirt, she was standing barefoot and bare-legged in his salon.

Of all the miserable luck!

"Business?" Lavinia queried doubtfully. "What kind of business?"

Leigh was spared a reply by Derek's timely re-entry. "Musical business, of course," he assured the reporter with his charm in full swing. "Leigh is a very talented artist in her own right, Lavinia. We're planning to do some work together."

Leigh glanced at him angrily but his expression remained guileless and easy. She checked her own telltale features and slipped back into her mask of a smile.

Lavinia White clapped her hands ecstatically. "Is that true, dear? How wonderful! And I'm the first to know!"

Leigh hesitated only slightly. If she said yes, she was cornered. She would have to complete the project with Derek. But if she said no . . . she knew her presence could only be construed in one way and her face and name would appear shortly in magazines across the country in a not-very-flattering light.

"Yes, Miss White. I started something with Richard several years ago and Derek thinks it's worth picking up again. Actually, we're not sure yet. We met on this today for the first time . . ."

"Leigh is overly modest," Derek said. "Her work is excellent and we're going to plunge right into it."

Leigh could almost feel bars closing in around her. How had she allowed all this to happen? Her headache was becoming acute. She felt as if a thousand drummers were playing a march behind her eyes. "It was nice to see you again, Miss White —"

"Lavinia."

"Lavinia, but I think I'll excuse myself. I've had a long day and —"

"A terrible headache," Derek supplied sympathetically. He had gotten his own way, he could afford to be magnanimous. "Do go on up to bed, Leigh. You certainly look like you need some sleep."

"Oh, must you?" Lavinia wheedled.

"Yes, she must," Derek answered firmly. He grinned amiably. "Leigh has a rotten temper when she's overtired."

She was tempted to slug him despite the reporter's observant eyes. Her face was strained from the effort of maintaining her false smile. "I am frightfully tired. And I'm not exactly dressed for tea or cocktails!" She shook Lavinia White's hand briefly and attempted to walk across the room nonchalantly. "Good night!"

"Good night, Leigh," Derek called. His eyes followed her up the stairway and they were gloating and triumphant. She returned his stare with shimmering venom until she could no longer see him. Damn him straight to hell! she thought balefully. He would find out just how bad her temper could be in the morning!

But her troubles for the night were still not over. She grimaced as she remembered that she had also bolted the hallway door to her room. She tried the knob anyway, but as she had expected, it was locked tight.

She wasn't going back downstairs. Not for anything. Sighing with exhaustion and resignation, she tried the door to the next room. It opened welcomingly at her touch.

She didn't switch on a light. Her body and mind ached and all she wanted was the solace of sleep. She walked in the dim light until she found the bed, pulled back the covers, and collapsed. She hoped, as she drifted quickly and mercifully into a sound doze, that Emma wouldn't mind terribly that she had made a mess of two rooms. . . .

Chapter Three

She was dreaming, and it was a pleasant dream. She was floating on an azure sea, kissed by the sun and caressed by the breeze. The water lapped by her side in perfect tranquillity, a feeling of relaxation to be matched by none. Overhead white clouds moved across the sky in soft, billowing puffs; they seemed to reach down and cradle her with a tantalizing warmth. . . .

She hurled herself up in the bed with a gasping cry. She was being touched and it wasn't by clouds. There was a body beside her!

She heard a muttered oath and then an impatient movement. Light flared through the room from a bedside lamp and she found herself face to face with Derek.

"You bastard!" she hissed, shaking so with surprise and anger that her voice wavered even in its harshness. "You are incredible! Get out of my bed. I know you're capable of dirty tricks, but this is too much. How dare you? And you have the nerve to condemn me . . ." Her words trailed away, not because she had run out of venom, but because he was staring at her very peculiarly and not saying a thing in his own defense.

"Would you please get out of here?" she begged in exasperation and confusion.

"I'd be happy to, madam," he replied with maddening deliberation. "Except this is my bed that you are in."

If a bomb had fallen in the middle of the room, she couldn't have been more shaken. She stared back at him helplessly, her eyes registering dismay as she remembered how haphazardly she had chosen a place to sleep. "Oh, Derek . . ." she stammered, venturing to glance around the room and note that the dresser was neatly covered with his toiletries and that the half-opened closet door displayed rows of pressed shirts and trousers. If only she'd turned on a light! "Derek, I am sorry. My door was locked, you see, I mean both doors . . . and I didn't want to come back downstairs, and — and, well, I am sorry."

"Don't bother to be sorry," he drawled lazily. His curious look had become speculative and his eyes, golden with sardonic amusement, roamed from her mane of sleep-tossed hair, to the deep vee created by the open buttons of the tailored shirt, and down to the long slender length of bare legs displayed beneath the tails. "Finding you in my bed has been a surprise, but a most pleasant one." He ran a finger along her kneecap.

Leigh pushed his hand aside angrily. "Damn you, Derek, I explained what happened —"

"Yes, I know." He smiled calmly. He was propped on an elbow and rested his head on his other hand. "You picked this room by chance."

"Yes!"

"Oh."

"Oh, yourself, and take the fast route to hell," Leigh snapped irritably. "Yours is the last bed I'd crawl into on purpose."

"Really?"

He posed the word like a perfectly polite question, but Leigh could sense the stifled laughter he was containing. She attempted to rise, only to discover she had one foot still caught in the sheets. With impatient force she ripped them aside, making a far worse discovery. Derek slept in the nude.

As Leigh gasped in an echo of horrified embarrassment, Derek chuckled, not in the least disturbed by the events that were mortifying to her. "Control yourself, love!"

he mocked. "I'm not going anywhere."

Fury choked back any reply Leigh might have made. She emitted a low growl, hurriedly tossed the sheet back over his bronze body, and unscrambled her own legs to make a hasty retreat. But in redraping her unexpected bedmate, she had retangled her own limbs. Her efforts did little but land her unceremoniously on the floor.

"Poor Leigh!" Derek taunted, rolling across to gaze down at her pityingly. "Doesn't seem to be your night, huh?" He patted the bed invitingly. "Why don't you give up this ridiculous charade of touch-me-not chastity and get back up here?"

"This isn't a charade!" Speechlessness deserted her as she shouted into his smugly leering face. "I don't like you, Derek, is that so difficult to comprehend? I don't want to be near you. I don't want to be in this house and I particularly don't want to be in your room and I especially don't want to be in your bed! I —"

She was rudely interrupted as Derek's hand clamped over her mouth. Then, with one swift movement, he was on top of her, and when he spoke, his eyes blazed into hers and his voice was a wrathful whisper.

"You, Mrs. Tremayne, are a perpetual liar! When I kissed you earlier, love, you

certainly responded. With amazing eagerness and expertise, I might add. Of course, you have had your share of practice."

The scathing things she had to say in return were effectively muffled by the force of his hand on her mouth. She twisted her head and struggled and writhed in a frenzy of energy born of anger so intense it filled every nerve and limb of her body. All to no avail. Between the confinement of the sheets and his rock-muscled strength, she was helpless. All she accomplished was to bring them closer together, to dislodge more of the thin material that was all that separated them and bring more flesh against flesh.

Finally she lay still, spent, frustrated, and frightened of the growing heat between them. She closed her eyes, refusing to meet his. When she had been quiet for several minutes, he took his hand from her mouth. Yet he didn't move. She opened her eyes imploringly.

"Derek, please, let me get out of here."

Her answer was an unyielding stare.

"Damn it, Derek, you are a crazy man! Why are you doing this when your opinion of me is so poor? I might be contaminating!"

"I find you very desirable."

"But you hate me!"

He shrugged. "Like you said, all black cats look alike in the dark."

"I'm not your average black cat, remember? I was Richard's wife, the cold, cruel mercenary."

"Richard has been dead a long time."

"And you still haven't forgiven me!"

Derek went on as if he hadn't heard her. "You responded to me, Leigh."

"But I didn't want to! Don't you understand?"

"No, love, I don't. There's a chemistry between us. Nice and normal. Two consenting adults —"

"No!" Leigh was close to tears. Moisture gleamed on her eyelashes. "Please?" A sob caught in her throat. If he didn't release her soon, she would be seduced by the nearness of him, by the raw masculinity she knew could become so demanding and possessing, yet tender. "Please, Derek."

He sighed and rose nimbly to his feet, wrapping the sheet decorously around himself as he did so. He extended a hand to help her up. "Get back in bed," he said. "There's nowhere else to go, at the moment. The room keys are in the kitchen somewhere, and it could take me the rest of the night and half of tomorrow to find them without asking Emma or James where they are. None of the other rooms are made up. Emma believes in making up a bed fresh when a guest arrives." He turned and stalked toward his closet.

"Where are you going?" Leigh asked hesitantly.

His back was to her and she saw his shoulders rise and fall in an unconcerned shrug. "It's almost five. I'll make myself some coffee."

"Five? It can't be!" Leigh exclaimed.

"Well, it is. I guess we both slept quite comfortably for some time before discerning one another's presence." He pulled a shirt and a pressed pair of jeans from the closet. Turning to glare at her impatiently, he added in a growl, "Go back to bed. Get some sleep."

Leigh pushed a billowing strand of hair behind her shoulder and remained standing awkwardly. "No — no, Derek," she stammered. "I'll go back downstairs. This is your room."

"Get in bed," he said firmly. "Unless you want me to put you there."

She hastened to obey. Their recent, bruising, crossed-swords encounter was too fresh in her mind to chance arguing further. Pulling her pillow to her chest, she watched as he obtained underwear from a drawer and headed for his bathroom, unwittingly admiring the span of his tanned shoulders as she did so. When the door had closed behind him, she glanced nervously about the room, focusing on the green luminescent face of a clock radio as she scanned it. It wasn't almost 5:00 A.M., it was only 4:30. She gnawed on a nail indecisively as she waited for him to re-appear. When he did, she plunged quickly into stilted speech.

"Derek, I, uh, I really don't feel right about kicking you out of your own bedroom. This bed is king-size, and we did sleep well for hours before discovering one another. I mean, we could both stay on a side and go back to sleep." She shimmied as close as she could to the edge. "See?"

He laughed. "Are you serious?"

"Yes, I am."

Rubbing his chin absently, he thought over her suggestion. Then he tossed the sheet he had been trailing to her. "Thanks. I'll admit I'm not crazy about early hours." He tossed off the sneakers he had just donned and crawled back into the bed, safely clad in his jeans and shirt. He switched off the light and settled in.

There was silence for a time and Leigh believed he slept. All that she could hear was their suddenly loud breathing and the howling of the wind. She curled into her pillow, but sleep wouldn't come.

"Leigh?"

She would have feigned sleep, but his question in the darkness startled her so badly that she jumped.

"What?"

"I'm sorry."

The gentle tone of his voice tore through her defenses as none of his harsh jeers could. The tears that had threatened before fell silently down her cheeks and she fought for control to reply.

"It's all right."

She felt his weight shift and then the touch of his finger on her cheek. She stiffened as his arm then came around her, drawing her to him.

"Don't," he said softly. "I'm not going to hurt you."

He didn't, but held her close instead, smoothing her hair with a lulling tenderness. She began to relax against him and her tears subsided. As the wind continued to howl, she drifted back into a contented sleep, dreaming again of white puffy clouds and a beautiful azure sea.

The sound of the wind, which had helped put her to sleep, also awakened her. She blinked the fuzziness from her eyes, yawned and stretched, and bolted up as she remembered the night. A quick look about assured her that Derek had arisen earlier and left her. At the foot of the bed lay the box with the second set of clothing he had purchased for her. She smiled with appreciation, then bounded to the window to strip away the curtains and view the action of the ferocious howling.

The sky was dead gray and the palms dipped so low from the screaming gusts that their thin, spidery leaves brushed the ground.

If they weren't in for the full strength of the hurricane, they were still in for some rough weather. The pool, she saw, was being drained, and as she watched, a flurry of activity became apparent. She heard a multitude of masculine voices, among them Derek's. The house was being battened down for the approaching storm.

She turned on the radio as she washed and dressed, hoping to catch a current advisory. She breathed a sigh of relief as she learned that Key West had been spared a direct hit; the hurricane had chosen a path across the central Keys and had taken its toll as far north as Marathon and Largo. It was now moving overland in a strange westerly pattern. It was hoped that it would wear itself out in the dense Florida Everglades, but warnings were up from Miami to Daytona and the north of the state was on hurricane watch.

Leigh tied back her hair and hurried downstairs. Even seeing it, she had not realized the brunt of the wind until she stepped out on the patio and was backed into the wall of the house. Aware now, she moved carefully across the pool area and out to the lawn, stripped now of all rattan and wicker furnishings. Looking up at the house, she saw that all the windows were shuttered, including the huge plate-glass doors.

"What the hell are you doing out here?"

It was not the wind this time that forced her cruelly around but an irate Derek. His face reminded her of chiseled granite as she returned his glare rebelliously.

"Listen, Mallory, I know what I'm doing, I was born here. You're the transplant."

"Wonderful logic. Being a native gives you the right to be a fool."

"You're out here!"

"And I'm coming in as soon as we finish. Get back in the house!"

"I'm not on your payroll! You can't tell me what to do!" she retorted. That his words made sense was irrelevant. His attitude was appalling.

Derek stared at her for a moment, noting the stubborn set of her chin. He opened his mouth as if to speak, shut it, then muttered, "Ah, hell!" The next second he tossed her over his shoulder like a limp sack of potatoes and walked her back into the house himself.

"Damn you!" Leigh sputtered when he had dumped her roughly on the parlor floor. "You're nothing but a muscle-bound idiot! You can't run around treating people like this. You will get yours one day!"

"But not from you, Leigh, so don't worry about it," Derek said stiffly, glaring down at her ignominious position with glittering eyes. "If you'll excuse me, I was busy. Cheer up — maybe I'll blow into the sea."

He turned away from her lithely and strode from the room, leaving her on the floor. She scrambled quickly to her feet, knowing that he once again irked her into poor behavior. "I have to get out of here!" she muttered to herself. Nothing ever changed. They had slept together as friends, but the coming of the morning had cemented their enemy status.

Her stomach emitted a grumble and she realized she was hungry. The alluring scent of freshly brewed coffee led her to the dining room. As she poured herself a cup of the steaming brew from a silver pot, she frowned at the settings on the large mahogany table. There were four of them. She wondered curiously what other guests Derek had invited in the middle of a tropical storm.

"Leigh!" Her voice was called with deep and sincere affection and she turned to see Roger Rosello, the "Duke of Rose" as he was known with the band, the erstwhile drummer of the London Company.

"Roger!" she greeted him with equal pleasure. He was a slender man, short compared to the others at an even six feet, and very dark from a distant Spanish heritage. His disposition was eternally easygoing, and Leigh had always cared for him as she might an older brother had she had one. He kissed her unabashedly on the lips and held her at arm's length to survey her, his dark eyes bright.

"You look great, kid, how are you doing?" he said, a grin splitting his strong features from ear to ear.

"Well, thanks." Leigh smiled comfortably in return. "How's life with you?"

"Can't complain." He let loose her shoulders to pour himself a cup of coffee and direct her to a chair. "We've been working like crazy. Keeping the group afloat with Richard gone —" He cut himself off and cast an apologetic grimace at Leigh. "I'm sorry, I —"

"Don't be sorry, Roger. I'm used to talking about Richard." She put a hand over his. "And he's been dead a long time. You must know too that we weren't in a state of marital bliss when it happened. But I think I look at things very objectively now. I learned a fair amount of bitterness from Richard, but I think of him fondly, not painfully. He was a brilliant man, and he also gave me a great deal of happiness. We all miss him sorely, but he is gone."

"You are quite a lady, Leigh, you always were," Roger said admiringly.

"Thanks!" Leigh took a sip of her coffee and changed the subject cheerfully. "So tell me — not that I'm not delighted to see you — but what are you doing here in the middle of a storm?"

"I have a place on Star Island now too. Derek called to tell me that you were here and invited me over. Kind of a hurricane party, I guess."

"Oh?" Leigh raised delicate brows. "Who else is coming?" The other two original band members, Bobby Welles and Shane McHugh, also had homes in or around Miami to be near the recording studios. But she couldn't imagine them coming over in the current weather. They both had wives and Bobby was the father of a two-year-old daughter.

She was surprised to see Roger looking uncomfortable again. "John Haley," he said finally. In response to Leigh's puzzled expression, he added, "You've met him a few times. He was with an American group until it split up last year. He's an accomplished lead guitarist and flutist." He watched his coffee cup instead of Leigh as he continued. "We wanted to stick with the original foursome. Derek wouldn't think of replacing Richard at first. But you know" — he glanced up again with a rueful grin — "Richard and Derek were the talent behind the group. The rest of us are hangers-on. I don't know if you've kept up with us at all, but the first album we cut without Richard was rough. Then we did a concert tour and everything fell on Derek. He was half dead when we finished.

Anyway, we added John shortly after that."

Leigh traced a circle around her cup and chuckled slightly. "Roger, quit apologizing. I'm glad you've hired John. If I remember correctly, he is very talented."

"There you go, John." The voice, coming from the doorway, was Derek's. Beside him was the young man they had been discussing, John Haley. Leigh vaguely remembered meeting him on a few occasions, all of which had been pleasant.

"I told you," Derek continued as the two entered the room and he moved to the coffee pot, "Leigh wouldn't resent you for a second." He handed John a cup of coffee and indicated the seat across from him as he climbed beside Leigh and gave her a brittle smile that didn't quite reach his eyes. "She's not the type to carry, uh, grief too far."

Leigh was sure that no one else caught his sardonic implication, but she mentally devised ways to manage dumping his coffee all over his lap as she smiled back. Then she turned to John with sincere welcome, ready to dispel the trepidation that lurked unhappily in his cool gray eyes. "I think it's marvelous that you've joined the group, John. Richard admired you very much, and I'm sure he'd be happy to know that you were chosen."

The naked pleasure that streaked across the newcomer's pleasant angular features was ample reward for her honest words. "Thanks for saying that, Leigh," he told her quietly, and she was struck by the humble sincerity of his manner. "It's rough to try and take the place of a man like Richard Tremayne. Having your approval means a lot."

"Don't take anyone's place, John," Leigh said, touched by the eager and personable young man. "Be yourself."

"Well," Derek said, "now that this is all settled, let's eat. I'm starving."

Leigh watched Derek with more curiosity than ever as he rose and began to serve them all from the various chafing dishes on the table. What was he up to? It was, she realized, possible that her elongated stay was simple happenstance, and that Derek would have invited his friends and associates over anyway. But for some reason she didn't think so. It all had to do with a plan of his, and not knowing his motives made her very nervous.

"Shouldn't we all really be off the Island altogether?" she asked sweetly. "I understand these small islands can be very dangerous."

"This house has been here since 'thirty-eight," Derek replied, equally amiable as he served her a portion of eggs Benedict. "She was built to withstand the weather — rain, wind, even flooding. We're quite safe. You should know, Leigh. You never left Key West because of a storm."

She smiled vaguely and crunched into a strip of bacon. A point that had been bothering her suddenly came into sharp focus in her mind. Roger had said that Derek *called* him. When she had asked Derek to call her a cab, he had told her that the phones were dead. He was definitely up to something, and in all probability he *had* done the damage to her car!

She never had to do anything on purpose to retaliate. He spoke her name, and she had become so engrossed in her thoughts that she started violently, consequently carrying out her earlier plan. She knocked Derek's cup accidentally and the scalding brew indeed emptied into his lap.

He yelped and jumped to his feet as the burning liquid drenched through material and hit flesh. Leigh rose too, horrified. She had never truly meant to hurt him.

"Lord, Derek, I am so sorry!" she cried, chewing a knuckle with uncertainty. Should she try to help him mop up? She couldn't! Not where the coffee had landed!

"Accidents happen," he replied dryly, but the tone of his voice told her two things. He didn't think it was an accident at all, and he certainly didn't intend to let it pass as one when he got hold of her alone. "Excuse me," he said with clenched teeth, and she knew too that he really was in pain.

She watched him helplessly as he strode from the room, miserable at the turn of events.

"Hey, Leigh, sit!" Roger said sympathetically. He tossed his napkin on the table and stood himself. "I don't think it's all that bad. Don't look so petrified!" He squeezed her shoulder as he passed her and left the room.

Leigh sank back into her chair. She had lost all taste for breakfast.

"I hear you're an honest-to-God Conch," John Haley said, tactfully changing the subject and attempting to dispel the gloom that had settled. "I didn't know anyone was really born in Key West."

"Sure." Leigh smiled in spite of herself. "Key West is an old settlement. There have been Conches for several hundred years. Where are you from?"

"Midwest. A little town in the Nebraska

corn country. I enjoy trips back home, but I like the South." He grinned engagingly and Leigh decided he was a very attractive man. She would enjoy spending time in his company. Thank goodness he and Roger had arrived.

"I have a home in Atlanta, too, but you know that. I sent you an invitation to a party I had," John continued.

"Umm, I remember," Leigh replied, surprised she could sound so cool and remote. "I really haven't gone too far since . . . in the last year or so," she corrected herself. "It was nice of you to have thought of me."

"It was a good party!" John chuckled. "Some of the costumes were terrific. We had one real beauty, a gorgeous creature, and I never even figured out who she was and it was my party!" His chuckle expanded to an explosive laugh. "You should have seen Derek that night! He left with the lady and *he* never discovered who she was! The poor boy was fit to be tied. He tore Atlanta apart for a month looking for her."

Leigh forced herself to join his laughter. She was feeling a little ill, having forgotten that John Haley had been her host on that night. . . .

"It must have been a good party," she agreed jauntily. "I'm sorry I missed it."

"Missed what?"

A chill crept down Leigh's neck as Derek came back in, clad in a new pair of jeans. She again had the sensation that his golden eyes were seeing through her, that the light in them pierced straight to her heart.

"I was telling her about that party I had in Atlanta," John explained. "And the one who got away from Derek Mallory."

"Oh," Derek said, pouring himself a fresh cup of coffee and sitting, one leg casually draped over the other. He smiled noncommittally. "I still think I'll find the lady one of these days."

John laughed. "The man never gives up."

"No," Derek agreed. "I never do."

Leigh picked up her coffee cup but the liquid was splashing dangerously. She set it back down. "Can I bother one of you for a cigarette? I seem to have left mine upstairs."

Both men solicitously offered her their packs. As Derek was closer, she accepted one from him. He grinned at the slight trembling apparent in her hand as he offered her a light.

"Nervous this morning, aren't you?"

"Am I?" She inhaled and exhaled.

"Maybe. I don't like being confined."

"We'll get some work done and take your mind off the confinement then," Derek said. "Finish up your coffee and your cigarette and we'll get into 'Henry the Eighth.'"

"I'm anxious to hear this," John supplied eagerly.

Leigh's reply was for Derek alone. "I told you I didn't want to do the damn thing!" she snapped.

"And you also told our late-night visitor of the silver pen that you were here on business," Derek reminded her. His sensuous lips were set in a smile, but his eyes were narrowed and gleamed devilishly. His words had been part challenge — part warning?

Leigh stubbed out her cigarette and walked swiftly to the door. "I'll play what I remember, Derek — then you take it from there. I'm going home as soon as the weather clears. And I'm not coming back for months of work. Miss Lavinia White is going to have to write up whatever she feels like, which she probably will anyway!"

She briefly saw anger streak across Derek's face, hardening his rugged jaw, narrowing his eyes still further. But she didn't stay to receive an answer. Striding with determined and lengthy steps, she hurried through the salon and parlor, past the curving staircase and into Derek's office, where Roger already waited. Barely acknowledging him, she slid onto the bench and began to play idly with the ivory keys of the piano.

Derek was angry now, she knew, because she had been so rude to him in front of John Haley. But she was too inflamed to care. She knew that he had schemed the entire situation — plotting her arrival in foul weather, trapping her into agreement in the presence of Lavinia White, bringing part of the group to bear further pressure on her and to keep her from arguing with him. Well, on that score, he was wrong. She was past giving a damn who knew about their grievances.

And it was all supposedly over the music. That she still didn't believe. But if he wanted it, then he could have it. All she wanted to do was get away, get away from the man she hated so fiercely and loved so dearly.

She had lied yesterday. There wasn't a note in any of the songs that she had forgotten. She plunged straight in, mindless of the men who listened, heedless of the barrage of criticism that might follow. Her delicate fingers slid over the keys naturally, her voice rose high and low, clear and sweet. She played straight, locked in a little world of her own, and when she finished, the only audible sound was the call of the wind that raged outside the house around them.

It was Roger who spoke first. "Damn, Leigh! That's not just good, it's brilliant!"

"Bloody brilliant," Derek echoed quietly, and Leigh chanced a glance at him. His eyes had lost their golden glint and were dark with sincerity.

She shrugged, unable to cope with the unusual compliments. "It's all yours," she said. "Use it as you like."

"Tell me," Roger said, moving from the door where he had been standing when John and Derek had followed her into the room after her explosive departure. "Why didn't you ever sing with us before?"

Leigh laughed, honestly surprised by the question. "Because Richard always said I sounded like a dying frog!"

The three men in the room exchanged a glance that Leigh could not interpret. Derek cleared his throat and bent his lengthy frame to join her on the bench. "Let's try it again, shall we? I think I've got the chords."

Leigh was sure that he did. Derek could hear the opening bars of a piece and pick it up from that. "John," he continued, assuming consent by all, "my guitar is behind the desk."

They played the music again and Leigh was amazed at how good it all sounded, the two of them at the piano, John on the guitar, Roger tapping out the beat on his knees. Derek's voice, blending with hers, added the final touches. When they finished this time, she sat quietly staring at her hands, tense with an excitement she was afraid to feel.

"As soon as the weather clears," Derek said, "we'll fly down to Key West and pick up the original music. Then we'll get Shane and Bobby and start work in earnest."

Leigh swallowed and lowered her eyes. He was too close to be nice to her! She could feel his breath as he spoke, smell his warm masculinity and the light aftershave he was wearing.

She moved from the bench. "I'm thrilled that you all like it," she said. "And you're welcome to it. But no one needs to fly to Key West. I'll mail it as soon as I get back."

"What do you mean, you'll mail it?"

Roger demanded jovially. "You're in this too, my girl. We wouldn't do it without you!"

"Roger!" Leigh exclaimed. "That's sweet of you. But you don't need me. I can't play anything half as well as any of you do and Derek could write books on what I don't know about music —"

"You'll be singing with me," Derek interrupted.

Leigh gasped with amazement as she stared at him, stunned. He had to be joking! As long as she lived, she would never forget the things that Richard had said about her voice, never accept that they were anything but true.

"Come on, Derek!" she retorted. "Enough is enough."

"What did you do before you met Richard?" he demanded suddenly.

She stared at him with exasperation. "You know what I did! A group of us used to play and sing calypso music for tourists —"

"Exactly."

"I don't understand what you're getting at."

"Did anyone tell you you sounded like a frog then?"

"Don't you get it?" John Haley moaned.

102

"You were Richard's *wife*. He loved you; he didn't want you becoming involved with the band. He probably wanted to keep his private life private."

Had that been it? Leigh wondered. Had Richard's blustering, scornful criticism been part of a deep-seated insecurity? But why? She had never given him cause to doubt her. When she had filed for divorce, he had known exactly what her reasons were.

She looked to Derek and found him studying her inscrutably. He rose when he caught her return glance, stretched, and yawned as if he didn't want her to know what he was thinking. "Anyone for a game of pool? It must be getting close to lunchtime. Let's go play a grand championship and then hit Emma up for some sandwiches."

John and Roger likewise stretched and yawned and agreed with Derek. Leigh began mechanically to follow the two out the door, but Derek's grip on her elbow stopped her. "Go on," he said to John and Roger. "I'll play the winner. I need to speak with Leigh for a minute."

"You can let go now," Leigh said, looking pointedly at his hand on her arm as the door closed.

"Can I?"

She wasn't sure if he were amused or still angry.

"You want to talk — talk." She extricated her arm with a small jerk

"I want to know if this is settled."

"If what is settled?" She knew what he was talking about but she wanted to stall for time. Her feelings were confused. She knew she should simply get away. But learning that her work had merit and that she could be wanted for her own talents was exhilarating. As accustomed as she had become to Richard's fame and artistry, she had never imagined hearing her own voice on the radio, or seeing her own name in print.

"Dammit, Leigh!" Derek snorted impatiently. "Don't play games with me! Are you going to stay and see this through?"

"I — I don't know," she faltered.

"Why?"

"Why what?"

"Why don't you know?"

"Oh, Derek, what a stupid —"

"Not stupid at all!" he ejaculated, gripping both her arms and flinging her around to face him. "And I'll tell you why. You're afraid of me and that's stupid."

"I keep telling you you're as crazy as a June bug!" Leigh countered defiantly, her hazel eyes blazing. She didn't attempt to break his grip. "You tell me not to be afraid of you, but you're constantly throwing accusations at me or — or attacking me."

"Oh. And you're Madam Tact when you talk to me?"

"You started it all!" Leigh flared.

"And attacking?" He laughed dryly. "You threw your purse at me, you tried to slap me, and then you appear in my bed! Who's attacking whom here?"

"I —"

"And on top of all that, you make a sound effort to destroy my sex life forever by scalding me! Think of my poor parents! They would be heartbroken to think all chance of future Lord Mallorys was wiped out by a viciously thrown coffee cup!"

"Derek! Stop! I beg you!" He had to be teasing her, but she couldn't be sure from his unrelenting features. "I swear to you, it was an accident! I wouldn't have really harmed you on purpose!"

"Perhaps." The faintest ghost of a smile played upon the corners of his mouth. "But I owe you for that one!"

She was absurdly happy as he placed his arm around her shoulder and led her out the door. The idea tingled in the back of her head that Derek's attitude had improved because he slowly was coming to realize that Richard had been capable of telling less than the truth.

"You do want to work on the album," he said thoughtfully, as they followed the U shape of the house to the game room on the opposite side flanking the pool. "I can feel it, no matter what you say. So come on, commit yourself."

She hesitated no longer. "All right, I'm committed."

"Good. As soon as the roads clear, I'll drive to Key West with you and we can pick up the music and the things you'll need."

"I can drive back myself."

"But I don't trust you to return here. Anyway, I could use a few days' vacation. I'd like to do a little fishing and diving."

Derek, when he chose to be, was capable of selling air conditioning to Eskimos. Although she could hardly say they had come to any real understanding, Leigh was lulled into believing they could become, if not friends, at least amiable partners.

Until they neared the game room. Then he stopped her once more. "Oh, Leigh." He spoke as if in afterthought. "Stay away from John. He's just started with the group, you know, and I'd hate to have any trouble."

"John?" Leigh echoed dumbly.

"Always the sweet innocent!" Derek scorned her confusion. "You were coming on to him at breakfast. All those smiles and the shy encouragement. You keep forgetting — I know you!"

Leigh stood stock-still, her muscles wired within as fury boiled to her head with a dizzying pain. Her low, controlled voice was an amazement to her when she spoke.

"Derek, you do not know me at all, because you do not care to. But I'll tell you this, I won't stay away from anyone on your say-so! And if there is any trouble, I can guarantee you'll be the cause of it."

They stood for what seemed like forever, glaring at one another, both aware of the cocoon of hostility generated between them. Derek finally broke the heated silence.

"Well, love," he drawled. "Then I'll guarantee there won't be any trouble at all. I'll see from the beginning that I never give it a chance to exist!"

Chapter Four

The hurricane whipped and roared and wreaked havoc throughout the day, but by nightfall she had passed on, weakened as the eye itself had hovered inland, and only the outer circumference had played up on the coast. Star Island lost electricity, but few of the inhabitants suffered discomfort. Most had their own emergency generators, as did Derek.

Telephone lines, however, were down. The bridge was impassable. Property damage had been great in many places, but even in the smaller Keys, which had first been struck in the United States, no lives had been lost. A gentle toll for a hurricane of such force.

Leigh wandered from the house just as dusk was descending. The wild lashing of the sea had subsided to slow ripples; the merciless wind had died to a softly blowing breeze. Shades of crimson and gold streaked across the heavens, casting a glow of peace upon the battered land. The air was crisp and incredibly fresh, as it could only be after the cleansing effect of a storm.

She ambled idly down to the dock and sat despite the dampness of the wooden planks. She was glad to see that Derek's yacht, ironically called *Storm Haven*, had weathered the wind and thrashing sea remarkably well. She stood now like a regal lady, proudly silhouetted against the setting sun, rolling lightly in the lapping waves. Behind her the pale streams of a rainbow jetted in a magically disappearing arc.

Hugging her knees to her chest, Leigh watched until the sun sank into the sea. The day, after Derek's cryptic remark, had been a tense one for her. She had been careful to stay away from him, choosing to interrupt Emma and James in the middle of their gin rummy game and assist with lunch rather than enter the game room with Derek. She had played a game of eight ball with Roger when Derek had gone to radio the guardhouse and check on Tim and Nick, the generally invisible employees who nevertheless held considerable import as they manned the electronic eye and assured the safety of Derek's property and privacy and cared for the kennels.

When he returned, she yawned and excused herself for a nap.

She had slept for a spell, and when she awoke, it was to hear the rasp of the shutters being lifted. She knew then that the storm had moved on and crept downstairs to sneak outside alone.

"Not too bad, huh?"

She started and went rigid at the sound of Derek's voice. He had the terribly annoying habit of addressing her as if nothing ever went wrong between them.

"The damage here," he continued, taking a seat beside her and wincing as the dampness crept through his clothing. "I've lost a few palms, and the pool looks like a deserted shambles, but that's about it."

"Good for you," Leigh muttered. Maybe he could act like all was peaches and cream, but she surely couldn't!

"Nasty little witch, aren't you?" he queried lightly, hesitating over the "witch" with deliberation.

"Leave me alone," Leigh suggested, "and you won't have to hear any nasty comments."

"Can't leave you alone at the moment, love." He gave her one of his wide smiles, which sent a rush of unease trickling down her spine. It was not a smile one could trust.

"Well . . ." She dusted her palms on her jeans. "If you're going to sit here, I'm going to go back in the house."

"Oh, no, darling, let's stay out here a few moments longer."

Leigh was not alarmed at the sudden rise in Derek's voice, but rather quizzical at the out-of-character endearment. She arched a brow at him, ready to ask if he were feeling all right, when he swiftly reached out and drew her into an intimate embrace. She opened her mouth to shout her outrage, but he, sensing her intention and his own advantage, claimed her lips with his own, forcing her teeth farther apart with his steely jaw even as she attempted to bite him in a bid for freedom. Her hands were useless to her, for he caught them both expertly as he pushed her back upon the pier and held her secure with the weight of his torso.

As she struggled against him vaguely, she sensed that he was not kissing her for the pleasure of the experience. He made no effort to entice or to seduce her, but held her rigidly, tense himself, giving only a fraction of his attention to her. His eyes, like hers, were not closed; they stared intently toward the house, a direction from which she could hear the remote sound of voices.

It was an act, a carefully planned and staged act. She was supposed to be seen in Derek's arms, seen in a position where it would appear that she was perfectly happy, perfectly content, perfectly willing!

The remote voices became more so. In the distance she could hear a sharp click . . . a door closing. Derek removed his muzzlelike hold from her lips, but maintained his clasp on her hands.

She would definitely have struck him if she could have.

Her breathing was ragged and uneven from her struggles, her chest heaving with indignation, making her speech barely coherent, which might have been a blessing. The things she had to say were certainly not nice. She raved in gasps, trying to shout but unable to, casting upon him every name of abuse that would come to her mind. And he sat and stared and listened, never releasing his hold upon her a hair, never interjecting a comment of his own. She cursed him on and on, until her fury sputtered itself out in a final, enervating exhaustion. When she had spewed forth her last words of contempt and scorn, she felt as if she had just run the Boston Marathon.

And that, of course, was exactly what Derek had intended.

"Why?" she breathed, when she had drawn air again.

He shrugged, clearly amused despite the venom that had been rained upon him. "Nothing personal. I told you I'd make sure there was no trouble."

"I see," Leigh said icily. "This was a little act staged for John. But don't you think you're jumping the gun a bit? What makes you think John is interested in me anyway?"

Derek smiled nicely. "He's a man, a young man at that."

Leigh laughed, the sound dry and bitter. "What flattery! Every man is going to fall head over heels for me?"

"Like I said, John is young."

"No one here is young!" Leigh snapped. "I'm twenty-seven, John has to be at least thirty, and you, you —"

"Bastard?"

"Thanks, it will do — will shortly be thirty-seven! All adults! We're all capable of looking after ourselves!"

"It doesn't matter," Derek said indifferently, but there was a smug look, like that of a contented cat, in his eyes. "I won't have anything to worry about anymore."

"I see. John will think there's something between us."

"Isn't there?"

"Certainly. Dislike and bitterness." Leigh tried to shift but his weight and restraining hands still held her firmly. "Could you move now, please? Your little charade went off quite well. John and Roger are long gone."

"I'll move as soon as I'm sure you're calm," he replied flatly.

"Then you may be here a long, long time!"

"It's a nice night." Derek might not have had a care in the world.

Leigh emitted a low moan of exasperation. "What if I assured you that I have no designs at all upon John Haley? That I promise not to make a problem in any way for any member of the band?"

He moved one hand, securing both of hers in the other with a twist of a long finger, and scratched his chin, mocking her in slow deliberation.

"Well?" she demanded.

"I'm thinking." His free hand moved from his chin to her cheek and he traced the fine bone structure of her face and brushed aside a lock of loose auburn hair.

"You're quivering."

"I am not quivering!" she retorted, dismayed at the way her flesh so easily gave her away. "I'm shuddering!"

"That's not a shudder," Derek murmured in correction, his head lowering over hers. "It's a decided quiver. . . ."

It was indecent, Leigh thought vaguely before giving herself over to the delicious sensation, that anyone should kiss so well, that the mere blending of lips, the meeting of tongues, could destroy all rational thought, could create a boundless heaven of damp wooden planking. . . .

It was a very long time before she realized she was no longer restrained. His hands were too busy — exploring the form beneath the material of her skirt, enticingly creeping, touching each shivering rib, and molding over firm breasts that willfully arched to him — to be involved with keeping her in place.

And there was certainly no need. Her own arms had risen to embrace his back, to feel the warm, taut muscles there, to hold him closer to her as she mindlessly slipped into obedience to the demand of aroused sensations. Her fingers crept into his hair, tantalized by the clean crispness, delicately tracing the breadth of his chest to his flat waist, feeling keenly his heat through the thin material of his shirt. . . .

The pearl snaps on her shirt were coming undone, but she didn't notice, except, maybe, to appreciate the loss of their restriction. It had been so long since her flesh had felt his tender, sensual touch, so long since she had felt such delicious heat burn within her, the ecstatic fulfillment of longing, love, and desire. So right. So very, very right.

But it wasn't right. She loved him; he scorned her. The passion he showed her was just that. Desire, and the arrogant belief that he could use her and manipulate her as fitted his will.

His expert lovemaking — which had just allowed him to undo the snap of her lacy bra and to handle and tease the creamy mounds of her breasts and their rosy, hardening nipples — was skill, learned from years of practice. She, Leigh Tremayne, panting beneath his knowledgeable touch, meant nothing to him. Certainly not love . . . if anything at all, only revenge.

And what better revenge than to make her love him, need him, long for him with every fiber of her being? Then he could repudiate her — as she supposedly had Richard!

He was off guard now. She pushed him with all her strength and he went rolling over, grabbing for her instinctively. Together they plunged off the side of the dock — and into the frigid water below.

The storm had left the normally tepid channel as cold as ice. The chill stabbed Leigh through and through like the savage edge of a knife as she sputtered to the surface. They were not in deep water. Derek was standing as he shot her a furious oath and a glance more chilling than the water. He hooked his arms onto the dock and chinned himself up to shimmy back on the planking. Leigh couldn't stand, nor could she pull herself back up. She swam to where he now stood, hoping his wrath wouldn't be so great that he would leave her foundering in the cold water.

He didn't. His hand shot down and he cruelly pulled her up, his grip merciless, his expression shocked and livid. "What's the matter with you, woman?" he demanded, shaking with his rage, his eyes as gold and hard as newly minted pennies. "You're as hot as a coal one minute and the next . . . You're a vicious tease, just like Richard said!"

Leigh's mouth flew open with a stunned denial. Surely Richard couldn't have said that! "Derek, I —"

"You what? There is no excuse for you!"

"Don't force people and you won't get any surprises."

"Now you're flattering yourself! That sure as hell wasn't force!"

"But it was!" she cried. "It is force because —"

"Because you don't want me touching you?" He laughed, deep, disdainfully. "You are a perpetual liar, Mrs. Tremayne. You fit to me like a hand in a glove. You lie through your teeth, but your flesh and blood tell the truth." He pulled her inexorably to him and her breasts were pressed to his chest, forming to his heat and strength. He possessed her again with burning kisses that stripped her of will as they moved along her face and down the length of her neck to push aside negligently the wet clothing that covered her collarbone and shoulders. His hot kisses were not an act this time, but nor were they gentle. They had their revenge as they fastened upon her with humiliating ease, audaciously claiming her nipples and breasts. Yet Leigh was a spellbound captive, seething with horror at the realization that he could not help but see the physical response he elicited despite the roughness with which he used her. Her tremulous lips, her rigid nipples, her erratic, gasping breaths — were all dead giveaways.

Then he pushed her away. "So you don't want me, Mrs. Tremayne. I know it is not love for your husband that makes it so. It must be that your lover still waits in the Keys. The same lover for whom you cast aside Richard Tremayne."

Leigh was so stunned that she couldn't speak. And as she stood staring at him, her hair plastered against her face, her lashes dripping the saltwater, and her clothing in dishevelment, she began to understand. It had all been Richard. He had created fictions to suit his convenience. He didn't want her singing; he told her she sounded like a frog. He didn't want a divorce, but he wouldn't change his ways. So he blamed it on her. He told Derek the divorce was her fault — that she wanted it unconditionally; that she had a lover, rather than himself having several.

And she *had* filed the papers. Derek knew it. It was only natural that he believe Richard on everything else. Richard had been his partner, his associate, his lifelong friend.

Derek mistook the wide-eyed shock on her face as an admission of guilt. She knew

119

as his jawline hardened that he thought her surprised only at his knowledge of her affairs. His next words verified this.

"So you thought no one knew, huh? Sorry, I was the closest thing to a brother Richard ever had. He was a broken man, Leigh, he had to talk to someone. But don't become overly alarmed. I am the only one he ever talked to. And out of respect to Richard, I've never mentioned any of this before. When he died, I let the pretty lies go. I let the world go on thinking that Richard had been a happily married man, that his widow had closeted herself away in her grief, that she had stayed sweet and loving to the end. You're safe, Mrs. Tremayne. I am the only one who knows that Richard might have purposely gone off that cliff because the woman who he had adored and married cared only for his money and status and was using them to support a bum of a lover —"

Leigh slapped him with the strength of a madwoman. Had he not been so vicious, had hate not glittered so clearly in the gold of his eyes, she would have tried to explain, she would have told him they had all been duped. But what good would that have done? He would never have believed her. The only man who could have cleared

120

her in Derek's eyes was Richard, and Richard was dead. And now she understood with pathetic clarity what had happened, what had changed the kind and gentle man who had been her friend into a towering volcano of seething animosity bent on justice. She knew that the tender and caring lover she had had so briefly as another woman could never exist for her in truth.

A red mark was rapidly spreading across his cheek where she had struck him, but she didn't care. They couldn't be friends; they might as well be out-and-out enemies. "That's right, Mr. Mallory," she hissed furiously. "Wanton little me. I can't resist the touch of anyone male, including you, even though I do hate you with all my heart! But my friend in the Keys . . . well, he's terribly jealous and demanding and I do love him so I try to control myself. . . ."

Flippant anger was the wrong path to have taken. She stopped speaking because the wrath in his eyes and rigid stance was so murderous that she became frightened. "I told you, Leigh, never to slap me." His voice was as low and ominous as thunder. His fingers abruptly curled into the back of her hair so tightly that tears sprang unbidden to her eyes and she was sure that her scalp would shortly depart from her head. He swung her around in his punishing grip and shoved her toward the house. "This is your last warning — don't do it again."

There was no course for her but to head back inside with her chin lifted. Any further words between them could be deadly as well as futile.

He followed her back to the house, both dripping seawater. They met Roger on the patio, who said, "Bad time to be swimming," merriment playing in his eyes. "I came to warn you dinner was about ready, but . . ."

"We'll be right back down," Derek chuckled, throwing an arm around Leigh's shoulder. "We got a little carried away."

Leigh winced at his touch, ready again to do battle and set all records straight now that Roger was present to buffer her from Derek. But he was, again, prepared for the response he knew she would make. Her words were nothing but a gasp as he easily hoisted her into his arms and carried her to the staircase, his throaty, amorous-sounding laughter drowning out her gulping attempts to protest.

He took her to his own room instead of hers and dumped her on the bed, and when she indignantly tried to stand, he roughly threw her back.

"Just what do you think you're doing, Derek Mallory? You can't keep me away from the others forever! And when I do talk, you will be in trouble!"

"And you will look ridiculous!"

"Oh, and how is that?"

Derek took her chin lightly but with great menace. "Because, my dear, Roger and John are now thoroughly convinced we are having an affair. Flighty and pen-happy Miss Lavinia White will be thrilled to fill her magazine with the news of it; after all, she did see you in a state of undress! And —"

"Affairs end!" Leigh whispered defiantly. "And this one is ending right now."

"No, it's not!"

"Derek, you can't make me do anything! I don't care what anyone thinks or what anyone writes! All I want is to get away —"

"And that's the only thing I'll deny you!"

"Why?" Her single word was a cry of despair.

"Why do you think?" he demanded bitterly.

Tears sprang to her eyes and she choked them back. "You're trying to punish me for Richard, but Lord, Derek! I've paid for

Richard. You never gave me a chance! You don't know the half of it!"

"I know enough!"

"Richard has been dead a long time! Why now? Why?"

"Because you wouldn't have come before."

Derek uttered his statement dispassionately and finally left her on the bed to walk to his closet, choose a dry outfit, and begin to strip, apparently comfortable doing so in her presence. She glanced longingly at the door to estimate her chances of making a quick escape when he grated, "Don't try it. You'll be sorry."

She replied with a derisive, brittle laugh. "And what will you do?"

"Try it."

"I will, Derek, and if you touch me again, I'll scream bloody murder!" Leigh warned, tossing her head in her most contemptuous manner. She stood with disdainful grace, slowly, as if she thought no more of him than of a harmless fly.

She made it as far as the door. Then he was upon her in two easy strides, naked to the waist. The crisp mat of hair on his chest tingled through the soaked blouse that clung to her skin as he caught her and threw her back even more viciously than before. Caught in his viselike grip, she could only stare with disbelief as he quietly told her, "Why, Leigh? Why all this? Because of Richard, because of me, because of you. There was no judge and jury to take care of you on Richard's behalf. So it falls to me. Stupid, idiotic me. The one who praised you to no end, the one who envied Richard his beautiful and charming wife, the one who would hear no wrong until forced to see it all. You mocked Richard, Leigh, and you made an absolute fool out of me. None of which I ever wanted to believe!"

Leigh hung limp against him. The puzzle pieces were all fitting in, everything was in the open. Any mask of chivalry Derek had worn had been to connive her to stay where he wanted her.

"So what now?" she asked bleakly. "Why don't you just beat me up, macho man, and leave it at that?"

"Too easy!" he muttered.

"Then what?" she demanded flatly, no longer rebellious but tired. "You can't keep me forever to torture . . ."

"No, your sentence isn't life."

He left her again to finish dressing, sure she would not take off again. Leigh lay with her eyes closed, incredulous that he could think he could hold her against her will.

He came back to the bed and jerked her up by the wrist. "Let's go. You have to change before you get pneumonia."

"Wouldn't you like that?" she queried sweetly.

He ignored her and ushered her into the room next door, carefully locking the door after they had come through it. "Your suit is in the closet. Emma cleaned and pressed it." He leaned against the door with crossed arms.

Leigh took her clothing into the bathroom and changed quickly. She brushed out her hair and repaired her makeup. When she emerged, Derek was still against the door, exactly as she had left him.

"Now, Mrs. Tremayne," he said coolly, "the choice is yours. If you walk down those stairs like the nice little lady you always purported to be, the night may go well."

"And if I don't?" It was all too absurd!

"Then you take your chances!" Something in his expression caused her to pale perceptibly. "Let's go."

She wondered as she preceded him downstairs how she could have managed to become part of the nightmare she was living. There had been moments at first, she was sure, when Derek had truly gentled toward her. He knew Richard had lied about a few things! The scene in the office had assured her of that. But now, now it seemed he hated her more than ever. The violent rumblings of hostility he had barely concealed at Richard's funeral were erupting like the lava of a volcano.

Dinner, which she dreaded, went amazingly well. Derek slipped back into his mask of conviviality, and became the perfect host. It was an easy meal, comfortable, made so by the bantering between the three men who worked together and who, in that capacity, had shared in one another's lives to a deeper extent than family. Roger was the main entertainment for the meal, telling funny tales of early experiences. Leigh began to wonder how the conversation would have gone had Richard been present instead of she, if the four men would not have fallen into ribald jokes and laughed the night away, eternal friends and conspirators of the night.

They wandered into the game room after dinner, where Roger came upon Derek's picture albums. He ensconced himself into a well-padded couch with Leigh and went through them as Derek and John shot pool.

The albums were dated, and Roger started from the first year that the group, then shy and awkward boys, had first started playing together. They appeared in black velvet suits with ruffled white shirts, their hair — daringly long for those days! — curling over their collars.

"James put these all together for Derek, you know," Roger mused, as he and Leigh chuckled over the old pictures. "Staid old James! Pretends he can't stand the music but he bristles with pride over Derek anyway. I wish I had had a James!"

They moved on through the years, looking at remembrances of both the professional and private lives of the London Company. The boys in London, Glasgow, New York, Paris, and so on. Roger with an Orange Bowl Queen, Shane with the Italian girl who would become his wife, and then, Richard and Derek and herself, playing in the surf behind her father's house. Richard . . . tall, slender, handsome, his eyes as blue and light as the surf, his face as endearing and sincere.

Pictures followed of their wedding, Richard, the groom, Derek, the best man, Roger, Shane, and Bobby as ushers. Leigh, a very different Leigh, a bright, beautiful, and radiant bride. Derek, a Derek tender, admiring, respectful, kissing the bride. . . .

Pictures could be painful. Leigh stretched and snapped shut an album. "Those were fun to go through, Roger," she said, standing to uncramp her legs. "They made me feel drowsy, though. I think I'll go on up to bed."

"Don't go yet," Derek called. He paused and surveyed his shot, chalked his stick, and deposited the eight ball in the corner pocket. "Emma was making us some Irish coffees and scones."

He smiled at her caressingly and she smiled back with twisted lips. She wasn't up to arguing with him tonight, or putting any of his threats to a test. "Irish coffee sounds nice."

And it was very nice. They sipped it out on the patio, the breeze having lulled pleasantly. Except for the visible damage to the palms and other plant life, the storm might never have existed.

Derek sat beside Leigh, his arm around her shoulder or his hand resting on hers. She didn't fight him; she was too tired. Tonight the game was his. She could almost ignore the light touch of his long, strong fingers.

"Irish whiskey," Roger mused, thoughtfully scooping his whipped cream with a swizzzle stick. His gaze suddenly focused on Leigh. "Weren't your folks Irish?"

"My father was," Leigh replied, idly chewing on the plastic of her swizzle stick. "My mother was Welsh." She started as she felt a spasm surge through the hand Derek was holding.

"McTigh!" He sounded as if he were choking.

Leigh was puzzled. "Yes, my name was McTigh. But my dad was very Americanized. You two know yourselves how easy it is to gain and lose mannerisms and customs! Don't you agree, John?" She laughed. "Why there were times I would have sworn Richard came from southern Georgia rather than London!" She couldn't begin to understand Derek's reaction to the conversation. He had met her father!

"Yes, I'm sure we could all pass as Americans by now," Derek said absently.

"I didn't say that!" Leigh chuckled. "You've picked up a lot of American expressions, but it's obvious you're British every time you open your mouth."

"Just like everyone knows I'm an American!" John supplied. "Even though I'm with the London Company now."

"You know," Roger reflected, leaning his chin in his hands, "we need a name for

John. Remember, Derek, when we started the band how we all had the little names printed on our cards? You know what I'm talking about, Leigh. I'm the Duke of Rose, Richard was the Wizard of Oz, Bobby, Sir Robert, Shane, the King of Hearts, and Derek, of course, Lord Mallory. What could we have John be?"

"Something high-sounding too!" John chuckled.

"But American!" Leigh interjected. The liquor was numbing the pain she had been feeling and she was beginning to enjoy herself.

"American . . ." Roger said thoughtfully. "Chief John?"

"Too plain!" John protested.

"The Governor? The President?" Leigh was thinking American.

"How about the Pied Piper?" Derek suggested, apparently involved with the conversation although his eyes still seemed slightly distant and oddly speculative as he watched Leigh. "Pied Piper. For his flute."

"That's it! I love it!" John Haley decided jubilantly.

"And now . . ." Derek sipped at his warm glass and brushed at the mustache that no longer existed. "We need one for Leigh."

"But I'm not with the group!" she cried.

"You will be," he corrected. "For the next album."

"True! True!" Roger delightedly tapped on the aluminum table. "Maybe the Wizardess of Oz?"

"No!" John protested quickly, and Leigh saw by the glance he exchanged with Roger that he was reminding him Leigh now belonged with Derek. "No, Leigh should have her own special name."

"Wonder Woman?" Roger tried.

"Ugh!" from Leigh.

"There's always the Black Widow," Derek proposed innocently. "But actually, I have a better one, The Lady of the Lake. Medieval and quite fitting too, considering Leigh is only truly happy in or around water."

Leigh shrugged and downed the tail end of her drink. The peculiar look Derek continued to give her was making her terribly uneasy. If she were an animal, she would be sniffing the air for danger.

"Sounds good," she said, suppressing a faked yawn. "I think I will go up now, if you all don't mind." Without meaning to, she glanced at Derek for his approval, wincing inwardly at the amusement and spark of triumph that sped briefly through his eyes.

"I'll walk you up," he offered.

"You don't really need to," Leigh demurred. If she could only move quickly enough . . . She planted a light kiss on top of his head and waved jauntily to Roger and John. "You all stay and talk!" She scampered into the house, confident that Derek would not follow now.

But he did. He was knocking at her door even as she closed it.

"What, Derek," she moaned, throwing it back open to admit him.

"I just wanted to tell you good night and" — he leaned against the door with sardonic amusement — "good show."

"Isn't that what you want?" she jeered.

"Umm . . ."

"Well good night and thank you." Her sarcasm ruffled him not at all. He continued to watch her, curiously, as if he had seen something new. Then he chuckled. "Good night . . . me lass!"

He left, closing the door with a snap behind him.

"What ails that man?" Leigh wondered aloud irritably as she bolted the door uneasily. She shook her head with disgust and changed into a shirt with little thought. She was so tired! She had been at Derek's for less than forty-eight hours and he had totally exhausted her.

Yet sleep, when she had tucked herself into the four-poster, was hard to come by. Her eyes kept flying open as her mind raced on.

Derek was blatantly out for revenge. And in a way she understood his feelings. She could well remember the way Richard could tell a story, the way he could make you almost believe it was night when it was day. And she, like a fool, had fostered Derek's belief in her coldhearted infidelity by her impulsive angry words.

At moments, she thought wistfully, Derek honestly wanted her. She instinctively knew when his touch was sincere. But, and she hardened her heart, Derek honestly wanted a number of attractive females. He was a womanizer, like Richard.

Games. All they did was play games together. Hers had been one of unrequited love and desire; his was based entirely on bittersweet revenge. He was making all the plays; as yet, she had hardly had a turn.

But the chance for her move would come. And when it did she asked herself wryly, which way would she turn?

Chapter Five

"You're a lucky girl, Leigh. Like those model types in the soap operas who manage to waken in perfect form."

Leigh rapidly blinked the sleep from her eyes to stare wrathfully at the figure casually seated, hands around knees, at the foot of her bed.

"How did you get in here?"

"Key, of course. I own the house, remember," Derek replied.

"Good," she told him curtly. "Go find somewhere else in your house to sit!" She turned her back on him and added, "I thought it would take you a day and a half to find the key."

"So it would, except Emma found it for me."

Traitor! Leigh thought silently. "Could you go away, please? I'd like to go back to sleep." She pointedly closed her eyes.

"What? More sleep? You've already slept half the day away!" Derek proclaimed, ripping her covers rudely from her. "Come on downstairs, my love, we're having a party and you're the hostess for the day."

The drapes went flying open and Leigh blinked again, painfully, as she forced her lids up and acknowledged from the angle of the sun streaming through the window that it was late in the day. She groaned and buried her face in her pillow. "Go have your party without me."

"No way, love. It's a work party." His voice had taken on a crisp and authoritative edge. "Get your sweet body up and moving. My office."

Leigh jumped up seething as her door slammed after his exit. She had had just about enough of Derek Mallory. She glanced out the window with narrowed eyes. The sun was brilliantly shining; only a slight breeze whispered through the foliage.

She was getting off Star Island, this morning, alone.

Determined, she showered and flung open the closet door to find the beige suit that she had worn the night before. It was gone. In its place hung a new assortment of clothing — blouses, pants, and three dresses. It infuriated her further to realize that someone had been very busy in her room while she had thought she was sleeping in privacy.

But if she wanted to leave the room, she had to dress. She chose jeans and a short-sleeved gold-threaded blouse, a comfortable outfit for a drive. Then she moved purposefully down the stairs. She didn't expect to find her own car waiting outside, but if Derek had arranged a "party," then the phones had to be in order and the bridge passable. She would call a cab, and fly back home. The Audi could be picked up later, when Derek had tired of his game.

The receiver was wrenched from her hand before she had dialed the first number.

"What do you think you're doing?" Derek demanded hotly. He must have moved like an Indian into the parlor, she hadn't heard a sound.

"Leaving."

"The hell you are!" Derek propelled her toward his office. "Shane and Bobby are here. We're going to work."

They did work, for hours. Derek barely allowed her a cup of coffee before they began, which startled no one. He was a strict taskmaster, which they all knew, yet he demanded nothing of anyone he wouldn't give himself. Leigh knew that he was most rigid on concert tours, when he jogged five miles a day and refused even a glass of wine with dinner.

They broke late in the afternoon, and when they did, Leigh was trapped thoroughly in a way Derek must have known she would be. Blue-eyed Shane McHugh and eloquent Bobby Welles were, if possible, more enthusiastic about the project than Roger and John had been. They, too, insisted that Leigh must be a part of her own work. Bobby filled her head with images of videodiscs and Shane suggested that they could film a complete program to be sold to various subscription television networks.

"Of course, Leigh," Derek said with sickening sincerity, a look of understanding sympathy on his face that should have won an Emmy, "we will not force you to join us. We can always hire Samantha Downing to do the female harmonies and sections."

Leigh tensed in her chair, but smiled brightly. She would never let Derek know how deeply his barb had struck. Samantha Downing was a singer with a voice like a crystal angel. She had also been one of Richard's first outside "affairs." Did Derek know that?

"That won't be necessary," Leigh said.

Derek had sprung another trap, but in this instance her pride forced her to walk into it open-eyed. She batted shy, conniving lashes. "Since you all are willing to bear with my inexperience, I'll thank you for your patience and enjoy the ride!"

It was the perfect response. The cluster of males, minus Derek, hastened to scurry to her and assure her they were more than willing to be as patient and helpful as she would need.

The real party, which followed their rehearsal, was an enjoyable occasion, even though Leigh knew that all present were secretly mulling over the new relationship between her and Derek with glee. What could be more fitting? Derek, caring for his best friend's widow. Leigh, who knew them all, who loved and understood music, with Derek. . . .

Angela McHugh and Tina Welles had come over with Shane and Bobby and Bobby's little girl, Lara. Emma and James were off for the evening since Miami and the Beach had recovered quickly from the effects of the storm. They had, Derek informed Leigh as he escorted her into the kitchen to assist Angie and Tina, made a cute couple as they left for a dinner at Joe's Stone Crab, the proper Englishman and the plump American matron.

"The boys are barbecuing," Angie said as she gave Leigh an alarmingly happy hug. "So we're throwing together some salad and wrapping up some ears of corn."

It was easy, Leigh thought, as she chatted with Angie and Tina, to remember how nice it had been when they had all gotten together. She and the other two wives had become fast friends as had their husbands; they had enjoyed the tunes when they had been able to meet as a group, any set of normal couples leisurely whiling time away with amiable company.

The conversation between the women was general at first. Little Lara tottered among them, lisping but sweet as she broke in occasionally with her childish voice. She was a beautiful little girl, Leigh thought with a pang, but then she had beautiful parents. Beautiful, happy parents. Bobby Welles, she knew, could be set in the middle of a bevy of naked beauties and he wouldn't notice a one of them. He adored Tina. They had the kind of marriage Leigh had believed that she and Richard would have.

And it was beautiful raven-haired Tina who dropped their bantering chatter to demand, "Why didn't you keep in touch with us, Leigh? Angie and I both wrote . . ."

Leigh raised her hands helplessly. A painful spasm ripped suddenly through her muscles. For a moment she saw their last meeting clearly in her mind, like the slow-motion, brightly colored replay on a television set. Richard lay in an oak box while the birds sang and the sun shone; Derek stood beside her, though distant, a pillar of strength. Tina, Angie, Roger, and the others and a host of strangers to mourn the passing of a brilliant star moved by them, tears in their eyes, unspoken sympathy showing in their drawn faces.

Then they were all gone. All except her and Derek, and Richard between them in the dirt. Then Derek had broken. The towering, proud giant broke and tears came streaming down his face. Leigh tried to comfort him despite the gulf that lay between them. But he wanted nothing from her, he told her in no uncertain terms. She was, he railed, anger and hate returning his strength, a witch, a lying, hypocritical witch. He had had a few more choice words for her before turning on his heel abruptly and leaving.

"I — I needed some time," Leigh said lamely. Roger, as did Derek, had known trouble had stirred between Leigh and

Richard. But even he hadn't known about the impending divorce.

"Sure," Tina said, her voice husky. "But time does heal all wounds."

"Hey!" Angie declared, sweeping little Lara into her arms. "If we don't get this corn out we'll never eat! And I'm starving!"

"Starvin'!" repeated little Lara with round eyes.

Leigh chuckled and reached for the little girl, softly touched by the feel of her chubby hands. Would she ever hold such a wonderful bundle of love of her own? It was doubtful. She would be twenty-eight on her next birthday, not old — certainly! — but time was passing by.

"I'm starvin' too, Lara! Let's go hurry your daddy," Leigh said.

As the night wore on, Derek continued in his subtle ways to give the impression that he and Leigh were now a twosome. Tina and Angie would sometimes glue their heads together in soft conversation, and Leigh supposed they were happily considering the chances of a second marriage. She wanted to laugh bitterly. What would they think, she wondered, if she were to stand and calmly announce that Derek didn't give a damn for her, that the whole charade was some type of malicious revenge?

They would think she was crazy. Derek was displaying his complete, suave animalistic charm. He was devastating in the starlight, his jeans tight over his trim hips, his shirt casually unbuttoned and showing the breadth of his deep bronze chest. When he spoke and smiled, his teeth would flash white and perfect against his rugged jawline, his eyes would sparkle like gold against the copper of his strong features. His fingers often touched upon Leigh, awakening her every nerve, sending her into chills of trembling each time.

What if . . . she began to ask herself, what if she went along with his little game. How would he react if she pounced upon him in return, became in public the loving mistress he pretended her to be? She would certainly throw him off, and perhaps find out just what part this mock tenderness played in his ultimate plan.

She didn't have the nerve! She could act all she wanted, but Derek had the strength. He had the power, because he cared nothing for her while she . . . was going to do it!

She would beat Derek Mallory at his own game!

She might wind up shattered later, but he would never know it. He wanted to think of her as a conniving little cheat, well, by golly, that was exactly what he was going to get. He had said he desired her. When she finished with him, he was ping to go crazy with his desire. He wanted everyone to think they were together, she would verify that reasoning. And then she would turn on him, as he had turned on her.

She began with the subtlety he employed himself, fingering his hair as she jauntily checked on the barbecue, pretending to massage his back when he chanced to sit near her, even going so far as to pat his firm rear end when he passed her on his way to the cooler for another beer.

His stunned response left her hard put not to burst into gales of laughter. Unfortunately, her triumph didn't last long. Derek learned to stifle his surprise and in return dropped all pretense of subtlety. She learned abruptly that the tide had changed when she teasingly caressed his neck, only to be drawn into a long and barely controlled kiss, enjoyed with relish by the entire company.

As the fabled moon moved high over Miami, they moved the party inside. Leigh accompanied Tina upstairs to put Lara to sleep in her portable crib, then returned to the game room with the others. Derek caught her as she entered, and maneuvered her into a position where she half reclined against his chest. It was a loving scene, she thought ruefully. His hand moved along her rib cage familiarly and settled beneath her breast as he casually chatted.

"Oh, Leigh!" Tina impulsively interrupted the discussion on the light area damage of the hurricane. "It is so wonderful to have you here with us again!"

"It sure is!" Bobby echoed, hugging his wife closer to him.

"Wonderful," Derek repeated, and only Leigh caught the sardonic inflection in his tone.

Angela muttered something quickly to Bobby in the Italian he had begun to understand and then smiled at the group mischievously. "And so wonderful that it seems you will be with us for a long time, yes?"

An idea ripped madly through Leigh's head. It was the perfect time to call Derek's bluff. Did she dare? She giggled, thinking, the devil made me do it. True in a way. Derek was the closest thing to a real devil she had ever met.

"Oh, darling!" she crooned. "We should tell them!"

Derek jerked and stared down at her adoringly angled head, his eyes narrowing and his pulse suddenly increasing. "Tell them what, *darling?*"

"Really, Derek!" she admonished, pushing playfully from him. "He's so shy!" she exclaimed to the group, a very convincing, loving smile glued to her tolerant lips. She chanced a quick glance his way to find his jaw stiff and eyes glittering suspiciously. She plunged on quickly, "Well, darling, I think they should know." Her smile increased and she faked tremulous tears. "Derek and I are going to be married, as soon as we finish the new album."

Derek's muscles tensed as if he had been hit by a red-hot poker. She could feel the terrible steel coils of his thighs beside hers as the group went pin-dropping silent. Then Angela and Tina jumped to their feet simultaneously, followed by their husbands, to rush to her and Derek and voice their sincere happiness and congratulations.

Leigh felt the first horrible pangs of guilt over her ridiculous announcement. These people were her friends as well as Derek's.

There was no need to have involved them in their private problems, no need to have created such excitement, which could only be dashed cruelly upon the shore of lies. At least, she assumed, it would all be over quickly. Derek would now have to denounce her and she would explain it had all been a joke. . . .

But Derek did no such thing. After his initial astonishment, he grinned, accepted the congratulations of his friends, and eyed Leigh levelly.

"Really, Leigh!" he mocked her with silky tones. "Now that you've let the cat out of the bag, as they say, why should we wait till we finish the album? I never did believe in long engagements. I'm sure we can arrange something nice and suitable in the next few weeks."

It was Leigh's turn to be totally astounded. She couldn't think of a thing to say. Once more her move had viciously backfired. She could only sit and listen to the plans that ricocheted around her, suggestions from Tina and Angela, winks and chuckles from Bobby and Shane, heartfelt good wishes from John and Roger.

It was late when the company finally pulled from the drive. Leigh tried to escape Derek while he said his last goodbyes and to race up the stairway before he could catch her, but she never had the chance. He maintained an iron clasp around her until the final car, Roger's gray Mercedes, disappeared down the moonlit path.

"What's the hurry, love?" he demanded dryly as he felt her preparing to spring from him. "Shouldn't we be discussing our wedding plans? Or perhaps be wallowing in the ecstasy of our love beneath this silver moon?"

"If I'm with you, darling," Leigh retorted, "I'm already wallowing."

"Tsk! Tsk! That mouth of yours will get you into trouble one day," Derek warned, ushering her back into the house. "Go to bed. I want you up and ready by seven tomorrow morning!"

"For what?"

"The Overseas Highway has been cleared for traffic. I want to leave early."

"For Key West?"

"Yes."

"Why do you want to go with me now?" Leigh asked, her voice caught between bitterness and pleading. "You know I'll come back. You know that I want to do the album now!"

"You don't like Samantha Downing,

huh?" Derek shrugged indifferently. "It doesn't matter. You don't think I'd let my beloved fiancée take that long drive by herself, do you?"

Leigh breathed a sigh of disgust and gripped the banister of the stairway tightly. "I'm sorry I came out with that, Derek, I really am. I was sure you'd come out with the truth. But we have to stop this ridiculousness now."

"Maybe I'm really intending to marry you."

"Hell!" Leigh sniffed. "And I wouldn't marry you —"

"Or," Derek mused, ignoring her statement of derision, "maybe I just want to bed a hot —" He captured her hand in midair as it sailed toward him. "Or maybe I want to make sure your friend in the Keys hears about this. Maybe I want to meet him and be sure to let him know, after I blacken both his eyes, what it feels like when the woman you love jumps into bed with another man."

Anger surged through her like a rushing tide as she stood a prisoner of his encircling fingers. "You can say we're living together, Derek, or you can say we're engaged. Believe it or not, you won't be ruining anything —"

"Oh? You mean he doesn't care if he shares you?"

Leigh ignored that. "And you won't find anyone's eyes to blacken." He had begun to lead her up the stairs. "But my strongest promise is this, Derek Mallory, I will never jump into your bed!"

"Why not?" He was amused suddenly, chuckling. "You've jumped into it before."

"By accident!" Leigh exclaimed. "You know I was locked out! You know that I didn't know that was your bed!"

"Ah, but, love," Derek said gravely, "that's not the occasion I'm talking about!"

In a split second Leigh's hands became clammy; the hairs on the back of her neck seemed to stand straight with cold, creeping fear.

"What . . ." She was choking, her throat constricted. "What are you talking about?" That was better. Her demand came off with irritation.

"You don't know?"

"Of course not!" Good, she was indignant.

Derek smiled lazily, his eyes like some feline predator in the dim light "Maybe you'll think of it. Good night." He moved on down the hall to his own bedroom doorway. "Oh, Leigh, don't forget, seven A.M. And be ready, or I'll drag you out of bed and dress you myself."

"That should be a new one for you," Leigh muttered crossly beneath her breath. "I would imagine you're much more experienced with undressing women!"

He turned and she cringed, startled that he had heard her.

"I'm quite good at that, too, my love," he said gravely, a mocking smile stealing into the corners of his sensuous lips. "You'll have to try me sometime . . . again."

Leigh had nothing else to say. She slammed into her room, fighting the shakes as she tried to assure herself that she had imagined Derek's last word. He couldn't be referring to Atlanta, he couldn't be! If he had had any suspicions regarding her, he would have confronted her long ago. Besides, he was still determined to find his mysterious and missing date.

Uneasily convinced, Leigh drifted into sleep. Derek, she decided, before succumbing to the comfort of a restful blankness, had merely discovered a new way to taunt her. Her lips curved into a soft, groggy smile. Sticks and stones may break my bones but words will never hurt . . .

Darkness claimed her, shutting out any reminders of just how painful words could be.

As they passed through Homestead the following morning, the disc jockey's blaring voice from the Audi's AM/FM radio announced an uninterrupted hour of music by the London Company. Derek, driving, impatiently moved to change the station, telling Leigh sourly that he was not in the mood to hear his own voice.

"Leave it, please," Leigh requested. It was the newest album that would be played, one that she had purchased, but had not been able to bring herself to listen to yet.

Derek, softened perhaps by her politeness, shrugged. He wore dark sunglasses as he drove, preventing her from seeing any of his thoughts.

The album was a pleasant mix of light-hearted fast tunes and soul-reaching ballads. One was about a child, and as Leigh glanced at Derek he said yes, he had written it especially for Bobby about Lara. The next was a hard, fast piece, the type that toes automatically tap to, about a "vixen beauty" who lied and cheated her way from man to man. Leigh wondered if that particular song had been written with her in mind, but she didn't glance to Derek for confirmation and he kept silent.

The final song of the set, though, was the one that caused her heart to throb in fast-paced agony. She knew beyond a doubt that Derek had written it for and about his mystery woman. His voice filled the small Audi with agonizing clarity, husky with emotion.

I remember you like a golden sunset;
I remember you like a fireside.
Crystal dreams and emerald seas
Lord, love, how you please.
Silver lady of the night
Disappears with dawn's first light . . .

There was more, but Leigh blocked out the words. She lit a cigarette and stared out the window. They were losing the station anyway.

"It's good," she said dispassionately. "Very good. More 'solid gold' in there somewhere, I'm sure."

"Thanks."

They were passing the long strip of A1A that would deliver them into the Keys. Snowy egrets dotted the slender landscape, and out in the deep azure water a pair of cormorants hovered over the horizon, hunting their breakfast. Leigh turned slightly in her seat to watch a great white heron standing proudly on one pencil-thin leg as he majestically surveyed his surroundings. She spun back around; the Audi was slowing as they entered Key Largo. Derek turned off the road shortly.

"What are you doing?" Leigh asked, puzzled. "This is Pennekamp."

"I know where we are," Derek stated flatly.

"All right then," Leigh replied, growing irritated. "What are *we* doing *here?*" John Pennekamp was an underwater state park. It was a beautiful place, boasting miles of protected coral reefs. Leigh had come many times in her life and enjoyed them all. But what was she doing here now, with *Derek*.

"What do people usually do here?" Derek cross-queried sarcastically. "We're going to go snorkeling."

Leigh smashed out her cigarette and exhaled with exasperation. "You are a crazy man, Derek," she said, repeating an earlier observation. "I thought you were in a big hurry to get to Key West."

"No," he corrected, "I was only in a big hurry to get started."

"And we're going to have a terrific time, I suppose?"

"I would think so." Derek grinned boyishly. "We'll be underwater most of the time. You'll have to keep your mouth shut."

"Funny, funny," Leigh muttered. "I don't have a bathing suit. We don't have our snorkel gear —"

"They've a nice little shop here where you can buy a bathing suit and we can rent snorkel equipment." Derek set aside her objections.

Leigh went silent with a resigned twist of her shoulders. If he wanted to stop and take a snorkling trip, he would do it whether she agreed or not. Then a thought came to her as she glanced at Derek's dark glasses. He had probably worn them more to conceal his identity than as shade against the sun. She almost laughed aloud. A devious little plan began to hatch in her mind.

"Perhaps this is a good idea," she mused, keeping a small note of reluctance in her voice. He might become suspicious if she sounded too eager. They parked and she hurried out of the car. "Why don't you check on the excursions and I'll see if I can find a shop."

"Okay." Derek seemed pleased with her affable agreement, and he smiled almost tenderly as he watched her, his eyes swiftly raking over her auburn hair, glinting like spun gold in the sun, and her warm, thick-lashed hazel eyes. "Hurry up. I'll meet you by the rental window."

Leigh remained nonchalant and sedate until he disappeared from view. Then she rushed into the shop and purchased the first suit she could find in her own size, donned it hurriedly in the dressing room, and asked the kindly clerk for a public phone.

With feverishly trembling fingers, she called the local radio station and announced that *the* Derek Mallory of the London Company was at John Pennekamp Coral Reef State Park. To assure the validity of her statement, she even gave her own name, while pleading that it not be divulged.

Then she smiled and hung up the phone, and slowly sauntered over to the rental window to meet Derek.

He came up shortly after she did, dressed in a pair of faded blue cutoffs. Leigh winced for a moment of regret. Clad so scantily, every rippling muscle, every tautly honed limb of his superb physique was visible. He would attract the attention of anything female whether his identity was known or not.

"We leave in forty-five minutes," he told her. "A four-hour trip, all right?" His handsome smile was sincere as he slipped an arm around her shoulder. "Then we can shower, dress, and stop by Marker 88 for a meal before driving on to Key West. How's that sound?"

"It sounds fine," Leigh murmured, feigning attention to the rows of flippers that hung in the window. She didn't want to meet his eyes. Guilt was taking a toll on her. Little pinpricks of uncertainty were telling her that Derek had really been trying to plan a nice day. They had both just found masks and fins that fit reasonably well when the first shout came, followed by a cacophony of noise and shrill screams.

"It is him!"

"There he is!"

"Oh, my God!"

"Derek Mallory in the flesh!"

Within seconds Derek was besieged in a sea of humanity, trapped between countless bodies and the rental window.

His scathing glance caught Leigh once before she was able to scramble away, and she began to regret her impish prank in earnest. The message in his glimmering eyes couldn't have been clearer had he shouted, *You'll pay for this!*

Leigh decided not to wait around to see how Derek would extricate himself from the quickly formed crowd of fans. She scurried down to the dock and searched out the excursion boat they were to take. Luckily, the boat was in her berth. Leigh hopped aboard and found a seat in the stern, hugging her knees and rocking nervously.

It seemed like an eternity before the boat began to fill. She was pulling away from the dock when Derek finally came on board, breathing heavily. He was forced to stop several times as he strode forward, caught by new adulation from those who were scheduled on the same trip. Finally, after speaking to everyone, he pleaded to be thought of as nothing more than a fellow passenger. Leigh watched him with grudging respect and admiration. He managed the situation very well, and she had to admit there was reason for him to be thought of so highly within the business and out.

"Cute!" was his short, terse word for her when he sank down beside her. "I'll thank you not to pull that again!"

She hesitated, then decided upon a play

for innocence. "Pull what again? I can't help it if you're a recording star and people recognize . . ."

His tense features and blazing eyes caused her speech to trail away. "Don't do it again, Leigh, I mean it."

She was relieved when it appeared he was going to say nothing more. But at the time he really couldn't have said much more. People were inching over to them, no longer determined to tear Derek apart as a celebrity, but fascinated that he was with them, an ordinary person out to view the beauties of the crystal waters. A number of young couples were on board and the conversation turned to water, sailing, snorkeling, and diving.

They dropped anchor and sent up their dive flag at the reef with the bronze statue of Christ set into the water. Derek and Leigh wet their equipment and donned it and plunged into the water, peacefully.

He was right; it would be difficult to argue with one's mouth in the water.

The bathing suit Leigh had so quickly purchased was a kelly green bikini. Occasionally Derek's fingers were pulled from hers to ripple down her back so that she might look in a special direction and view whatever it was he pointed out: a tremendous, friendly grouper, a colorful jellyfish to be seen but avoided, a school of brilliant yellow tangs. There was something very sensual about his touch in the water, something extra delicious about the feel of his extraordinary fingers.

Time passed quickly in the eerie little spot of oceanic heaven. Derek motioned her to bring her head out of the water and then suggested they move over to the statue before it was time to go back. Leigh nodded happily and followed him with a stiff kick of her large black flippers.

The others were leaving the statue as they approached it. Leigh inhaled for a deep dive and plunged through the fifteen feet or so of water that would bring her to the base of the bronze Christ. Then she slowly swam up its length, curious as ever about the beautiful piece of art sitting in the coral reef. Suddenly she felt Derek behind her, his hands moving along her waist to her rib cage and on to her back. She didn't fight him; the silky sensation was wonderful and besides, how far could he push in the middle of the reef with scores of people within forty feet of them? At the moment, she thought, he was welcome to be a bit amorous. . . .

But he wasn't being amorous at all. He

160

and the seductive sea had lulled her into a false sense of security. The hand on her back was not loving but devious. It abruptly pulled the strings of the kelly green bikini top and pulled the entire thing from Leigh's body.

Leigh spun in the water but Derek was already a good ten feet away. She was running out of air, forced to surface. She kicked herself up and cleared her snorkle, glancing around desperately for Derek. He broke the surface too, shooting water from his snorkle, then laughing gaily as he caught sight of her furious, perplexed features.

"Damn you, Derek," she shouted, "give that back!"

"In time," was his cool, chuckled response.

Leigh struck out for him in the water and he didn't move. She lunged for his hands to find that neither held her bikini top. "Where is it?" she demanded breathlessly.

"All in good time," Derek replied, a wicked grin planted firmly on his lips. Then his hands began to seek her. They ran over her velvety flesh, fixed upon the soft mounds of her creamy breasts, began to tease the rosy nipples that were clearly visible in the amazingly translucent water. . . .

Leigh desperately tried to pull away. "Derek, please!" she begged. "There are people . . ." Her struggles were stealing her breath as were his tantalizing maneuvers. "Please!"

He laughed again, a low, throaty sound, and allowed her to escape.

Then he calmly turned and began to swim slowly back to the boat.

"Derek!" Leigh screamed. He couldn't really be doing this to her, leaving her half naked to return to a crowded boat!

He slowly turned to her again, treading water, his brows quirked beneath his mask. "Yes?"

"Please?" she implored again. "I promise, I'll never play another trick on you again!" She waited, her legs flailing the water with strong strokes as he watched her, apparently mulling over a decision. "Derek!" she cried again, mournfully. The boat captain was calling his passengers back on board.

"All right," Derek called.

Leigh waited again, with exasperation. Seconds were becoming minutes and he wasn't moving.

"Throw it to me!" she exploded.

"Un-unh!" he returned with a shake of his curly head that sent a spray of saltwater flying. "You come get it."

Leigh swallowed with resignation and swam to him warily. "Well?" She hovered two feet away from him.

"Get it yourself," he taunted indifferently.

"Where is it?"

With half-closed eyes and a lazy drawl he replied, "Tucked in my pants."

Ten hours of straight sun could not have turned Leigh's body a darker shade of red. But his face was implacable.

If she wanted her green bikini top, she would have to get it herself. Cursing him all the while, she reached gingerly for his trim hips and delved into the faded blue cutoffs, praying she would touch nothing with her delicate fingers except her bikini top.

Chapter Six

"Calm down!" Derek ordered as she continued to curse him while trying to adjust the bathing suit. He was still annoyingly amused. "You'd better let me help you before the boat leaves without us."

Leigh stiffly turned her back on him and allowed him to retie the strings of her bikini. As soon as he finished, she kicked away, but a powerful kick brought him to her side and he jerked her back to face him. "Calm down!" he repeated harshly. "This evens the score. No more little pranks on either side. Agreed?"

"Ohhhh . . . agreed!" Leigh snapped. She really had no other choice. Besides, there could be more trouble back at the docks. Derek's throng of fans might be waiting for his boat to return. . . .

They managed to settle that problem back on board the boat. A sympathetic young man suggested Derek take his loud, tourist-type shirt and battered fishing cap and blend into their group. Derek gratefully accepted his offer, and suggested the convivial conspirators join them later at Marker 88. Needless to say, the man, his wife, and the couple with them were thrilled.

Derek did elude the crowds that had formed with the help of the captain and fellow passengers, promising them all autographed albums if they wished to call his agent. It was well known that he was a man who kept his promises.

An hour later they entered Marker 88 and were ushered to a rear table. The two young couples who had been so helpful on the boat joined them within a few minutes and Derek returned the borrowed shirt and cap. Leigh, who had hardly spoken to Derek since their encounter in the water, was surprised at how pleasant the meal turned out to be. They were bright young people, knowledgeable about many things, and conversation flowed easily. The waitress neatly rattled off the long list of special appetizers and entrees Marker 88 boasted daily, and between them they ordered one of everything. The snorkling trip and the sun and sea had left everyone famished, and Leigh, as well as everyone else, dived ravenously into clams casino, oysters Rockefeller, escargots in mushroom caps, and several other delicacies. She ordered a scrumptiously prepared Florida lobster for her main course, and ignored Derek's look of amusement when she accepted a taste of his king crab.

Sometime during the meal Derek mentioned nonchalantly that Leigh was Richard Tremayne's widow. Leigh shot him a look of pure antagonism as she then was plied with questions, polite at that, about Richard. She was treated to more sympathy, until Darlene, the wife of the man who had lent Derek the loud shirt, squealed, "Oh, my goodness!" She turned to her companions with wide, bright eyes. "Then we're part of an engagement party!" She looked at Leigh enviously. "I just read about it in a fan magazine. I should have remembered."

Leigh felt as if she were short of breath. "Read about what?"

"Oh, it was all in there!" Darlene explained giddily. "That you and Derek were disappearing for a private romantic liaison before working on something new and getting married."

"What —" Leigh moistened dry lips. "What magazine was this?"

It was, of course, Lavinia White's magazine. But where had she gotten the rest of

166

her information? Leigh allowed her suspicious and accusing gaze to fasten on Derek. He met her stare noncommittally, but she knew then that he had been the one to fill in all the blanks.

Derek ordered another round of drinks, and Leigh sipped hers slowly as the talk swirled around her. Damn him! she thought, for at least the hundredth time. And she had felt guilty over the trouble she caused him! Well, Mr. Mallory, she said silently, watching him covertly from the shade of her lashes, the hell with being "even"! You haven't begun to see trouble yet! She downed her vodka and tonic in a single swallow.

It was growing late when they finished their leisurely meal and split company with their still awestruck new friends. Leigh was dismayed as she tripped over the gravel in the drive on their way to the Audi to discover that she had been angrily drinking too fast. Derek gripped her elbow and ushered her into the car.

"I'm going to drive!" she muttered, further annoyed to find her speech slurring. "I have to drive! I have to drop you at a motel and —"

"You're drunk," Derek said flatly, "and you're not driving. And I'll be damned if

I'm staying at a motel!"

Leigh carefully enunciated her words when she spoke again. "I'm only a little drunk." She winced. She hated people who drove when they drank. "Okay, you drive. But you can't stay at my house. My housekeeper doesn't live in. The Casa Marina is a beautiful place, people come from all over the world —"

"I'm not staying at any motel," Derek repeated firmly. He flashed her an evil grin. "I'm staying with my beloved fiancée."

Leigh opened her mouth to argue but yawned instead. The food and drink and sunny exercise were combining to drain her of energy. Night had fallen and the lights of the Overseas Highway were mesmerizing her. Before she knew it, her eyes closed, her head fell to rest on Derek's shoulder.

She awoke with a start to feel motion and Derek's strong arms around her. He was carrying her up the path to her house.

"I need the key," he said as he noted her open eyes.

Leigh fumbled in her bag, which Derek had deposited in the curve of her stomach. "You can put me down now," she said. "I'm awake."

"But not terribly with it!" Derek chuckled.

With one hand he took the key from her fingers while still holding her and inserted it dexterously into the lock. He kicked the door open and switched on the lights, then proceeded through the living room to the bedroom she had shared with Richard.

"I don't sleep in there anymore," Leigh protested thickly.

Derek's arms stiffened around her. "Where do you sleep?"

"The next room," she murmured. She was so sleepy!

He moved on down the hall and pushed the door open with his foot. Dim light surged in from the hall so he didn't bother with another switch. He walked straight to the bed and deposited her in it. Leigh immediately began to curl into the comfort of her cool sheets. But she wasn't left alone. Derek was unbuttoning her blouse and pulling at her jeans.

"Don't!" she objected weakly, fighting for consciousness. "Please!"

"Please, what? You little fool," he muttered harshly. "I'm not doing anything, but you can't sleep like that."

"But —"

"I'm not going to see anything I haven't seen before," he interrupted.

She fell silent, a limp rag doll as he

hoisted her about to remove her clothing down to her brief panties. Then he tucked her into the covers and walked briskly to the door. Leigh struggled to sit up.

"Derek?"

"What?"

He was silhouetted in the doorway, his handsome form like a classical sculpture.

"Thank you," Leigh whispered, a catch in her throat.

"For what?" There was a rapidly beating pulse apparent in his neck.

Leigh licked her lips to speak. "For helping me. I did overdo it." She couldn't tell him what she was really thinking. *For not pushing or taking advantage when I'm so terribly vulnerable!*

"Yeah." The door was closing. "Good night."

Leigh rose bright and early, strangely cheerful. She threw back her drapes and tilted her chin to drink in the morning sun, then quickly dressed. She ambled into the kitchen to start coffee, but found that her housekeeper, a Cuban woman named Maria Lopez, had already done so. She heard jaunty Spanish singing coming from the living room and hurried out to say hello.

"Ah, senora! It is nice to have you home!" Maria exclaimed joyfully. She gave Leigh an unabashed, motherly hug. Her voice took on a tone of reproach. "You did not say you'd be gone so long." She shook a stubby finger and sniffed. "And who is that man sleeping in the guest room?"

Leigh stifled the urge to chuckle. She was twenty-seven years old, but Maria often treated her like a young girl in need of a duenna.

"That's Derek, Maria, didn't you recognize him?"

"Senor Mallory?" Leigh resented the obvious pleasure in her housekeeper's redundant question. "Oh! How very nice!"

Leigh had tossed her length into a comfortable Victorian love seat but she rose again restlessly. "Yes, how very nice, Senor Mallory." She fingered various knickknacks as she glanced around the room. She had furnished it, like the rest of the house, with Victorian and other turn-of-the-century pieces to match its gingerbread facade. The home, although new, had been copied after those in the old town, down to the widow's walk that stretched around the second-story circumference. The only difference with her "conch"-patterned house was that all the living area was on the first floor; the second floor was filled with musical instruments and recording devices. She didn't use the floor much anymore, but she had always been loathe to change it.

She set down the sand dollar she had idly picked up. "I'll go start breakfast."

"No, no, senora!" Maria dropped her dust cloth and started to bustle for the kitchen. "I will start your breakfast! You have just come home!"

Leigh's protests that she needed something to do went unheeded. Maria, promising exquisite Spanish omelets, shushed her out of the kitchen. Leigh sighed, accepted a cup of scalding black coffee, and wandered out the back door.

Leigh's "backyard" had always been a source of joy to her. Her home was as secluded as possible for the small but bustling island of Key West, set on the gulf side on a spit of beach called Blue Lagoon. And it was indeed blue. Shockingly so, against the bleached white sand, shells, and coral pebbles of the shore.

She walked aimlessly down to the water, beckoned by its still tranquillity. Reaching the edge, she kicked off her shoes and sat, and allowed the quiet tide to ripple over her toes. What am I doing? she asked herself with a hint of desperation. *Why am I allowing Derek to walk all over me?*

A large gull swooped down beside her, warily out of reach, and eyed her speculatively. Leigh laughed as she watched him comically twist his head and beak. "You think I'm a fool, too, huh?" He cocked his neck again at her voice. "Sorry, buddy," she told the bird. "I haven't a thing on me to offer you."

A piece of fish went flying over her head and the gull greedily and expertly caught it with his extended mouth.

"I take it this guy is a pet," Derek said, sliding next to her in the sand. He waved a plastic bag of fish heads and tails in front of him. "Maria greeted me with a spat of Spanish, stuffed this in my hand, and pushed me out the door."

Leigh chuckled. It was amusing to think of tiny Maria pushing a giant like Derek anywhere.

"No, he's not a special pet. None of them are. They come and go, but they all seem to know this is a good place for a handout."

She glanced at him quickly, then turned her concentration to the gull. The musky odor of his aftershave that she was coming to know so well could rattle the pace of her blood by itself. Looking at him, dressed, like a tourist in shorts and a knit shirt, was something she wasn't up to yet. His eyes were becoming too intuitive, his masculine face and form too dear. If she weren't careful, she would forget that his motives were to make her pay . . .

"So." She briskly stood and dusted the sand from her cutoffs. "What are we doing? When do you want to start back for Miami?"

Derek tossed another fish head to the nosy gull. "In a few days. I want to spend some time here."

"Doing what?" Leigh demanded crossly.

"The usual things one does in Key West," Derek replied complacently. "Fishing, boating, sunning . . ."

"You live in Miami," Leigh reminded him. "You can do all that there."

"Star Island is actually Miami Beach."

"Pardon my mistake."

"I want to go sit in Sloppy Joe's bar like Hemingway and sip cold beer. I want to take the Conch Train and listen to the tales about the pirates. I want to hit all the super seafood restaurants and visit Audubon's house. None of that, my love, can be done in Miami or Miami Beach."

"But, Derek" — Leigh was both confused and exasperated — "you've done all that before!"

"I want to do it again," he said firmly.

"Well, go on," Leigh said, "have a good time."

One arched brown brow raised high. "You, dear sweet, are going to do it all with me."

"Oh, no I'm not!" Leigh retorted. "I'm not in a touristy mood."

"Then get into one."

"Aren't you afraid I'll call another radio station?" she taunted.

Derek pretended to consider her question. "No, I'm not afraid." He flashed her a pearly smile. "Because, Mrs. Tremayne, should such a thing happen again, it will be more than a bikini top you find yourself bereft of, and whatever I might have you will not get back."

He was dead serious in spite of the deceitful smile and Leigh knew it. "I told you I wouldn't pull any more pranks anyway," she muttered, summoning a shade of dignity to saunter toward the house. "I'm sure Maria must have breakfast ready by now," she flung over her shoulder.

Typical of Derek, he forced Maria to join them in the omelets. He then plied her with teasing questions about her life, asking about her fisherman husband, her three daughters and two sons. Maria in return blushed like a young girl and giggled giddily as she gave her replies, responding with pride when it came to her children.

"José is in medical school now at the University of Miami," the middle-aged matron told him proudly. Her loving gaze slipped to Leigh. "Thanks to la senora here." Her big brown eyes grew wide. "It is so high, so very, very dear to pay! But Leigh . . . she tells me it is nothing."

Leigh, sipping her coffee, wished that she could fit a muzzle over her housekeeper's mouth. But what could she say? Maria had no notion that Leigh wanted Derek to know nothing about her finances.

"More coffee anyone?" she hopped to her feet to interrupt the flow of conversation. "More toast?"

"No, thanks," Derek barely glanced at her. "I'm enjoying my chat with Maria."

Leigh didn't want to hear anymore. "I'll clear the table, then. When you're ready to go, I'll be out back."

Leigh cleared the few dishes, which looked as if they'd already been washed since Maria really did make an exquisite Spanish omelet, and picked up a horror novel to take to the sand. She settled by the shore, lit a cigarette, and tried to absorb herself in the chilling pages.

The effort was no good. Black ink bluffed upon the white pages. She should be adamant about not going, she told herself, still staring at the book but not seeing a word. The truth was, she wanted to go!

"Hey, Leigh!" he was calling her from the screen door. "Ready?"

She scrambled to her feet. Derek was telling Maria not to worry about dinner as she re-entered the house. Maria demurely thanked him and waved them both out to the Audi.

Derek had been to the four-mile island many times and knew exactly where he was going. "Conch Train, first, okay?" Leigh nodded.

They spent an hour on the "train," listening to the bold and adventurous story of Key West's history. Their guide was excellent; she made the pirates and scavengers come alive in color, sometimes dashing, sometimes downright despicable. She talked about Henry Flager's railroad and the hurricane that had destroyed it. They passed Old Town and the western tip of the island and Leigh's father's house.

"Do you still own the place?" Derek asked her.

"Yes," Leigh replied simply. She would never sell her father's house although she would probably never live in it again. It held too many special memories for her.

"Let's stop by when we get off the train," Derek suggested. Leigh glanced at him suspiciously, but he was wearing his dark glasses and she couldn't read a thing from his tone.

"Why?" she asked bluntly.

Derek shrugged and lifted a hand in a casual gesture. "I'm feeling nostalgic, I guess. I remember the good times I had here talking with your father."

"I remember . . . You got along better with my father than Richard did." Leigh attempted to sound nonchalant, but her heart was racing. Why, she wondered, would a trip back to the old house mean anything to Derek? What was he up to?

Fifteen minutes later they were standing on the trellised porch and Leigh was nervously fitting the key into the lock. Derek's hands were in his pockets as he surveyed the exterior.

"It hasn't changed a bit," he observed.

"Not in two hundred years," Leigh commented dryly. She pushed open the door and entered the den, feeling the same surge of emotion that never failed to pulse through her when she came "home." The house was the embodiment of her childhood; a happy time, when she was as free as the gulls that soared the blue skies and as blissfully ignorant. Her world had centered around the sea and her doting father and growing up on the island had been everything a child could ask.

"Not a bit," Derek repeated idly. He brushed past Leigh and ambled slowly around the room, allowing his long fingers to glide lightly over various of her father's "treasures": carved ships in blown glass, porcelain figures of the sea, delicately sculptured meerschaum pipes. He glanced at Leigh suddenly. "It doesn't make you sad to come here, does it?"

"Sad?" Leigh echoed. A tender smile curved its way gently into her features. "No. My memories are very precious. I think I'm lucky to be able to afford to keep the place." Leigh turned abruptly from Derek and walked over to the grand piano and ran her fingers nervously over the keys. Why had she been so stupid as to make a reference to money? Derek would surely come back with something about Richard's legacy. The afternoon, which was going so pleasantly, was sure to be ruined.

But Derek made no sardonic reply. Instead he motioned her past the stairway to the door that led to the beach. "Let's sit out on the sand for a while. I want to talk more about your dad."

"Why?" Leigh mouthed, as surprise prompted her immediately to accept his outstretched hand and mechanically allow him to lead the way.

He answered with his usual haphazard shrug. "Because I want to understand more about you. And him."

Leigh stared at him with doubt, but his golden eyes were sincere and the hand that held hers was warm and supportive. There was no hint of demand about him now, just that openness that bordered on a true reach for friendship.

"I'll tell you about my life." She grinned shyly. "If you'll tell me about yours."

"Deal," Derek agreed. He unhooked the back latch and ushered her through to the weathered planks of the back porch and down to the surf. There he teasingly pushed her to a sitting position and lowered his large frame beside her with the easy grace of a great cat. "You first!" He laughed, his eyes calmly set upon the

Atlantic and the massive freighters on the horizon as he drew patterns in the sand in a random motion.

Tentatively at first, then with more ease, Leigh began to talk. She told him that she had no memory of her mother, but that her father had given her a beautiful picture of the woman he had loved, that he had spoken of her cheerfully and often. And he had been both parents to his only child, always there when needed, always willing to listen before commenting, always open to her thoughts and desires. "He seemed like a magician to me when I was little!" Leigh laughed. "So wise! He never raised a hand against me, but I was always eager to please him."

"Now that," Derek said, "is the secret I want to fathom."

"What?" Leigh asked, puzzled.

Derek shifted and lay back in the sand, his head resting in the palm of his hand, supported by a crooked elbow. "What it is that earns respect and love from a child." His eyes traveled from the water to Leigh's. "I didn't learn to love my own father until I met yours."

"You're joking!" Leigh gasped, shocked by his admission. She couldn't imagine not loving a parent.

"No, I'm not joking," Derek returned absently, cupping his free hand around a scoop of sand. "Both Richard and I had very proper parents. We were switched diligently for disobedience. And we became tough little hellions because of it. Oh, my mother was soft, but even she was under my father's thumb. I resented him for years. Now" — he grinned at Leigh — "I actually like the man."

His grin was contagious and Leigh laughed. "What did my father have to do with that?"

"I don't know exactly," Derek mused. "Showed me that people were different and often part of their heritage, I guess. Somehow, just being around him gave me a better understanding of other people." The tawny shade of his eyes darkened a shade but Leigh didn't notice. The conversation between them had lulled her into a sense of security. "Did he come to the States as a young man?" Derek asked, still playing idly with the white grains of sand.

"I think he was about twenty," Leigh answered innocently.

"He really had lost most of his brogue. Where did you learn yours?"

Leigh was now watching the freighters in their apparently slow drift across the ocean

182

and she replied without a thought. "When he was mad you could cut his accent with a butter knife!" She chuckled. "But I suppose I learned to affect the brogue from his mother. She lived with us for several years. They all emigrated together in a bad year for potatoes!"

Derek bowed his head, and Leigh was blissfully unaware of the secret smile of knowing satisfaction that flitted across his face. When he glanced at her again, his expression was bland and guileless.

"When I am a parent," he said, "I hope I can be like your dad." Dusting sand from his body, he reached a hand to Leigh as he rose. "He sure as hell did something right. He left you nothing but good memories, and yet they are more enviable than any of the Mallory fortunes."

"Wait a minute!" Leigh protested. "I still haven't heard —"

"Another day," Derek protested.

"But —"

"I still want to get a beer at Sloppy Joe's and I have some souvenir shopping to do," Derek interrupted impatiently. "Besides, you will meet Lord and Lady Mallory one of these days and that will answer all of your questions."

Leigh's further protests were to no avail.

Derek was dragging her back through the house and out to the car like a man who had accomplished a task and was now eager to move on to something else. Uneasy at his sudden change, Leigh searched her mind for a reason, but could think of nothing. Her trepidation over coming to the house with Derek had been groundless. He had been cordial and friendly the entire time. Glancing at his rugged profile as they drove back into town, she began to relax.

"With a childhood like yours," Derek said suddenly, his tone light, "I'm surprised you didn't want children."

Leigh bristled immediately and felt her spine stiffen like a rod down her back. It was coming. Another reference to how she had failed Richard.

"I did want children!" she snapped, turning on him. "But I'm not going to sit here and try to convince you that it was always Richard who was too busy! It's really none of your business and you're going to believe what you want anyway."

"Hold it! Hold it!" Derek laughed. "I'm not accusing you of anything. I was merely curious."

Leigh stared at him, her mouth still open. Finally, she managed to shut it and lean back into the seat, bewildered. Not only was he instigating pleasantries, he was actually refusing to argue with her when she sprang at him!

He remained completely pleasant as they reached Duval Street and ordered beer at Sloppy Joe's, the corner bar made famous by Ernest Hemingway.

"One would think this was your first trip here," Leigh told him as she caught a stray strand of hair blown aside by the huge ceiling fans.

"I know," Derek replied, sipping his beer and licking the foam from his lips. He was wearing the dark glasses again and Leigh found his thoughts impossible to guess. A smile tickled his lips. "Just wait till we hit the souvenir shops! I'll look like I'm fresh off a boat!"

Leigh smiled tentatively in return. As the fan-cooled air stirred around them and the blazing sun shone from the street, they chatted on idly, combatants mellowed to a state of truce by the easy, laid-back atmosphere of the "live and let live" Key colony. After a multitude of discussions that ranged from the best eating fish to the world economy, and after her third beer, Leigh suggested that they should get going.

"If I sit here any longer," she said and chuckled, "I'll fall asleep on you again."

"You're cute when you sleep," Derek replied, and Leigh could not tell if he mocked her or not.

They spent another hour on Duval Street so Derek could comb through the shops. He bought jewelry to bring back for Angela and Tina, fine pieces made of coral and turquoise, toys for Lara, T-shirts and other trivia for the boys in the band, a watch for James, and perfumes for Emma and Maria.

"When you buy souvenirs," Leigh commented, "you don't mess around!"

Derek shrugged casually. "What good is money if you can't spend it for pleasure?"

"Some people pay bills," Leigh replied tartly.

"True." He adjusted his purchases in his arms, pushed the large stuffed dolphin he had bought for Lara toward Leigh, and started down the street to the parking lot where they had left the Audi. He wasn't going to argue with her at the moment. "Come on! It's getting late."

Leigh gripped the fuzzy dolphin and hurried after him. He was strangely quiet as he drove, his jaw squared and tight. As they took a wrong corner, Leigh assumed his self-absorption had caused him to lose direction.

"This isn't right, Derek," she said. "You should have gone straight."

"I'm not going to the house," he replied. "I want to stop by the cemetery."

Leigh fell silent along with him, her skin prickling uneasily. At the wrought-iron gates, Derek bought a spray of flowers, then continued down the winding path until he parked and they walked the remaining distance to Richard's grave site. Leigh followed slightly behind Derek.

Derek placed the flowers in the two bronze vases that flanked Richard's final resting place.

"I'm surprised you didn't send Richard home for burial," Derek said matter-of-factly.

"Home?"

"Yes, to England."

Leigh frowned, puzzled. "Richard had no one left in England," she said. "No one close. . . ." For a few seconds she forgot that Derek was there and thought about the man who had been her husband and now lay beneath the neatly trimmed sod. "I think that's why he needed the adulation so much. He needed to be loved. He needed to be loved by many people." She realized suddenly what she was saying. She bit her lip and glanced at Derek nervously, expecting him to bristle and come up with a comment about her being such a poor companion that Richard had been forced to look for love elsewhere.

But Derek said nothing. He crouched down and dusted a cluster of dirt from the marble headstone. Then he rose and slowly began to walk away, back toward the car. He stopped suddenly and turned back to Leigh. "I'm sorry. Are you ready?"

"Yes." Leigh picked her way through the stones after him and hesitantly accepted the hand he offered her. Neither spoke again until they reached the house, then Derek, casting aside the gloom that had invaded them both, cheerfully commanded her to take a leisurely shower and dress up for the evening.

"Where are we going?" Leigh asked.

"Oh, lots of places!" Derek replied vaguely.

It was difficult for Leigh to control the excitement and happiness that were growing steadily within her. She tried to remind herself that Derek's kindness and friendliness could be a trick far worse than any of his cruelty. But all her stern warnings did little to dissipate the exhilaration that claimed her like a heady drug. The day had gone too well for her to maintain the guard she needed to resist him.

She bathed like a bride preparing for her nuptials, washing her hair with scented shampoo, filling the tub with an oil that lived up to its promise of leaving skin as soft as a baby's. The dress she chose was alluring, bold, and daring — a black silk that plunged to the cleavage of her breasts and completely bared her back. Side slits wavered teasingly as she walked, giving occasional glimpses of her slender legs. To complement the sophistication of the gown, she carefully pinned up her hair, not severely as usual, but in delicate, looping ringlets. She finished off with makeup applied heavier than was her custom, but right for an evening out.

At last she slipped into black, heeled sandals and spun before the full-length mirror in her bedroom, tense with anticipation. She bit a lip with happy excitement. Her eyes, bright with the cheer that could only come from natural elation, were enticing and adventurous. Her hair, high but soft, gleamed rich and red in its coils. The whole effect was perfect. Had she ever been beautiful in her life, it was this night.

Derek, handsome and elite and overwhelmingly masculine in black velvet, was waiting for her in the living room. His eyes roamed over her as she joined him, and for once they held nothing but sincere admiration. He sauntered over to her and offered her a sherry wordlessly. Leigh accepted the drink from him, then spoke quickly, afraid to let the drawing silence continue.

"You look dynamite! You should be in an advertisement for some ungodly expensive men's cologne!"

"Thank you. I'll keep that in mind if all else fails." He caught her arm and spun her in a circle. "May I return the compliment? If you were in the same advertisement, I guarantee you any male seeing it would run to the store in the middle of the night to purchase a cologne which could attract such a divinely stunning female!"

"Thank you," Leigh replied in turn. She sipped her sherry and withdrew her hand to wander idly across the room. "Have you decided where we're going yet?"

"Umm. I thought we'd have dinner at Pier House and move on over to the Casa Marina for after-dinner drinks and dancing."

"Nice," Leigh murmured. She sipped the rest of her sherry and inched toward the door. "I'm really starving tonight. We missed lunch, you know."

"Umm . . ." Derek repeated. The concealed amusement in his tone was evident by the golden twinkle of his eyes. "Nervous again?"

"Just hungry," Leigh lied. She was terribly nervous, not of Derek, but herself. She would soon forget that she didn't trust him. She opened the door herself and moved into the night.

Once they reached Pier House, a casually elegant dining place that overlooked the shimmering sea, Leigh began to relax. She was fine in Derek's company as long as they weren't alone. They chuckled companionably as they argued over appetizers, both having the inclination to order everything on the menu page. Then Leigh had difficulty deciding between the steak Diane and the lobster thermidor, and Derek laughingly said they would order one of each and create their own surf and turf. They split a bowl of conch chowder, smiling afresh as their spoons continually clashed.

A bottle of Dom Perignon disappeared along with their meal, which Leigh chose assiduously to ignore. She felt marvelous, and when they strolled along the moonlit beach before driving over to the Casa Marina, her steps were steady and her mind, although dreamily clouded, seemed to be functioning fine.

Derek was behaving like a perfect gentleman. He supported her as would any escort, but made no passes of any kind. The only time she fell into his arms was when they danced below the muted lights of the Casa Marina and drank sweet cordials into the small hours of the morning.

Leigh would later berate herself cruelly for her mistaken belief that the amount of alcohol she consumed was all right because she had been eating. She knew she had a low tolerance level, and she later realized Derek knew it too and knew exactly what he was doing as he kept her drinking and dancing, smiling all the while. By the time they left the Casa Marina and drove for her home, she was as relaxed and content as a well-fed kitten purring before a fire.

She was so relaxed that she accepted Derek's kiss with eagerness when they entered the house, accepted his arms around her and automatically brought her own to his back, her hands to caress and to luxuriate in the feel of his heat and strength. She was swept away by dizzying sensation as he lifted her easily and strode smoothly for her bedroom, lost in desire as he stripped aside the coverings and lay her pliant form down.

She didn't think as he pulled off her shoes, didn't resist as her nylons slid sensuously off her legs. It even seemed perfectly normal and right when Derek cast away his black velvet jacket and trousers, crisp silk shirt, and tight-fitting briefs. She knew every line of his magnificent bronze body, remembered with sweet anticipation the ecstasy of joining with his splendor.

He moved beside her and kissed her again, arousing her further with his probing tongue, bringing her body to burn as his own. His lips moved along the satin texture of her throat and she weakly protested, "We can't fall asleep. Maria will find us in the morning."

Derek was gently working on the clasp that held the black dress around her neck. "Maria won't be in tomorrow morning. I told her to take the day off."

Something snapped in Leigh's mind, a blaring suspicion that turned her heated blood cold. "You — you gave Maria the day off?" she repeated, stiffening within his arms despite his tender ministrations.

"Ummmm . . ." He was nuzzling her neck, but she wrenched away. It was all perfectly clear now. From the time they left the house that morning, his every movement, action, and gesture had been planned for just this moment. He had refused to argue with her, even over Richard, to lull her into a sense of comfortable trust. It had all been done just to get her into bed, to possess her, degrade her, use her, and hurt her — as she had supposedly hurt Richard.

"No!" she screamed. As much as she loved and desired Derek, as much as her body cried out for her to stay, it couldn't be this way. "No, let me go!"

His expression, she could see, even in the dim light, was stunned. Then anger slowly filled in as he observed her, propped up on an elbow, narrowing his eyes to cat gold and tightening his lips to a thin line. Freed from his weight and caressing hands, Leigh made a mad scramble to rise. He caught a handful of the black dress and it came apart in his hands as he jerked her back beside him.

"No, Mrs. Tremayne? I think not." His voice was a silky hiss. "But I am willing to hear about this sudden reluctance. You weren't in the least, uh, hesitant last time."

Hysteria was slowly claiming Leigh, creeping upon her as she read the determined intent in his eyes, felt the impregnable steel band of his arm around her.

"You're crazy, Derek, I keep telling you

that. There was no last time —"

He growled an impatient oath and his arm tightened. "What do you take me for, a fool? I know damned well that was you in Atlanta! You think I don't know your skin, your voice — Irish accent or not — your shape, your thighs, your every curve and every secret —"

"No!" Leigh cried again, horrified. "You're wrong! All black cats are alike in the dark! You told me so!" Her voice was rising shrilly.

"Not this cat, love, she has a streak of silver."

"No, Derek," she tried desperately for control. "Please . . ."

"If I remember correctly," he went on harshly, ignoring her protests totally, "you might even have been called the 'seducer' that evening. Granted, I was a willing 'victim,' but then, I don't really believe you're unwilling now."

"I am unwilling!" she shouted, grabbing for a last-chance stance of dignified hauteur. "Damn you, Derek, let me go this instant!"

His hold loosened slightly. "What is it, Leigh?" he asked coldly as she scrambled to her feet. "Do you make a habit of nights like that? Did you think it amusing to hoodwink me?" He was rising despite his nudity to face her. "Did you play that little disguise game and run around when Richard was alive? Is that how you met your lover?"

The situation didn't matter anymore. That Derek was standing menacingly before her naked, his every muscle taut and wired with tension, meant nothing. That she would be a fool to cross him never crossed her mind. All she felt was terrible, sick fury. And like a blind animal, all she wanted to do was strike out.

And she did. She flew at him like a wild thing, nails drawn, hands and arms flailing furiously. She was determined to pummel him to pieces, draw blood with her fists as he did with his words.

With agility and speed and raving fury, she delivered one blow. Then it was all over. "I've warned you a dozen times, love," he whispered coldly as he captured both her arms and held her tightly against him. *"I slap back!"*

And with a gesture that was actually more of a cuff, he did. Leigh went sprawling back on the bed, astounded that he would carry out such a threat.

He was beside her again before she could gather herself into more than a sitting position, gathering her to him in all his bronze glory.

"That's one lesson, love," he said, still in the deadly cold voice. "You're about to get another. Don't play your little teasing games with men, real men, unless you plan to carry them out. You came willingly into this bedroom with me tonight, and now, willing or not, you're going to stay here."

The remaining pieces of the black dress shredded from her body as he ripped it with one swift but powerful movement. Beams of moonlight peeped in from the half-open curtains, displaying her own naked beauty. She huddled, shrinking away from him.

"Derek!" Her cry was a broken plea as he collected her into his arms. "Oh, God, Derek, please, not like this!"

He went rigid for a moment, relaxed, stiffened, groaned. His face sank into the sunset of her hair. A shudder rippled through his length.

"No, my love, not like this. I would have you willingly."

But he did not release her. He began to make love to her again, gently and tenderly, caressing her with hands that softly explored the contours of her face, and more urgently discovered the intimate secrets of her breasts, her hips, and her thighs. And despite the emotions that boiled through Leigh, despite everything that had happened, she began to respond. She was the woman again who wanted nothing more than to touch him, to feel his embering flesh against hers, to wrap herself around him however briefly. . . .

He was creating a whirling vortex of pleasure she couldn't deny, a wonderful pleasure that only he could bring, because she could never, no never, no matter what he said, thought, or did, change the simple fact that she loved him as she had never loved in her life.

And in his arms, with his kisses and demanding, roaming hands consuming her, she soon forgot all else. Her fingers dug into his hair, she matched kiss for kiss. Woven surely into his web of passion, she lost herself in a returning, bold aggression, needing as he did to explore, to caress his broad chest with her lips, to taste the masculine roughness of his cheeks, to feel the muscular contours of his long back and sinewed thighs . . . steel that trembled with warmth and vibrancy at her touch.

When he finally took her, the sweet ecstasy was so great that Leigh sobbed with the shock and a shudder rippled forcefully through her. Their eyes met, and his were infinitely tender.

They were on a plain that surpassed all else, the special lovers inexplicably bound together, both aware of the magnetizing uniqueness that drew them together irrevocably . . . soaringly. . . .

That which had been sparked by anger became beautiful and rapturous. The night passed in a storm of tender passion, and as Derek had promised, Leigh came to him willingly. Again and again.

Whatever happened in the future, she could not regret this night, marked with turmoil as it was, when the cool breeze of the bay caressed the splendor of their love and a silvery moon looked down upon their union with a blessing.

Chapter Seven

The discordant jangling of her bedside phone woke her. The raucous sound, interrupting her from a deep dreamland, took awhile to penetrate.

"Maria will get it," she mumbled to her pillow.

The sound continued, bringing with it the reality and humiliating memory of her abandoned and painfully quick surrender. She groped a hand quickly to retrieve the receiver before Derek awoke, praying she could dress and escape the room without having to face him in the bright light of day. Maria, of course, would not be getting the phone.

Her hand touched flesh. Derek was already awake, answering her phone.

"Hello? No, don't hang up, you have the right number."

Leigh peeked as she heard a faint and garbled noise from the other end of the line.

"No, no trouble at all." Derek glanced at

her with twinkling eyes. "She's not busy, she's, uh, sitting right here."

Leigh pulled the covers to her chin and ripped the phone from his hand, gracing him with a malignant glare. "Hello?"

"Leigh? Who is that? What a marvelous voice! Is it . . . no! It can't be! I won't believe it! Or is it? Is it, Leigh? Is it Derek Mallory?"

The barrage of questions and exclamations came in a rush from her best friend, Sherry Eastman. Leigh had often grit her teeth over the last two years when Sherry raved about Derek, begging her to come to terms with him so that he would return to Key West and, presumably, Sherry's charms.

She lifted her eyes resentfully to Derek. He was fully dressed, and looked as if he'd been up for some time and already out on the beach. Covering the mouthpiece with her hand, she snapped, "Do you mind?"

He shrugged and sauntered out of the room, his eyes still twinkling mischievously, his grin still annoyingly smug.

"Yes, Sherry," she sighed to the phone. "That was Derek."

"Oh! Then things went well. Marvelous! When do I get to see him?"

"I — I don't know," Leigh hedged. The

last thing in the world she wanted to see at the moment was her best friend falling all over Derek. "I'll have to call you back on that."

"Leigh!" Sherry wailed. "Why don't I just hop over?"

"Not —"

"See you in a few minutes." The line went dead.

Leigh flew from her bed and into the shower. When she emerged, wrapped in a snowy towel, Derek was back in the bedroom, his long form draped casually over the foot of the bed.

Leigh scowled and studiously avoided his eyes. "Would you please get out of here?"

"Don't you think we should talk?"

"Talk! Good Lord! No!" Talk? In the full light of day? Look into his eyes as he mocked and made light of her?

"All right, we won't talk." He patted the bed. "Come here."

"No!"

"Then I'll come there."

Leigh gripped her towel tighter. "Derek, what happened last night —"

"Would have happened sooner or later. Sooner, if you weren't such a little hypocrite." He had reached her and his hands were running slowly along her arms. "You know me, and you know I get my way. You were also truly an ostrich with your head in the sand to believe I didn't know it was you at the costume party."

"It wasn't!" Leigh would never bring herself to admit it.

"I found the contact lenses this morning."

Leigh unwittingly focused her eyes on her dresser. The case was sitting next to her jewelry box. Why hadn't she gotten rid of the damn things?

"How dare you prowl through my room?" she demanded.

"Oh, I dare a lot!" He moved his mouth toward hers and his hand slid around to find the tie in her towel. "When I know I'm right."

His head jerked back up suddenly as the door bell began to ring.

"Who the hell is that?" he muttered fiercely.

"Sherry."

"Who?"

"Sherry Eastman," Leigh said faintly. She had been saved by the bell, but she wasn't sure if she was grateful for the interruption or not. "A friend of mine. You talked to her this morning, and you met her a few times — several years ago."

"Oh." He was scowling now as the bell insistently rang again.

"Will you go answer the door please."

"Maybe she'll go away."

"She won't go away," Leigh said firmly. "She knows you're here."

"All right," he grumbled, eyeing her sternly. "I'll entertain your friend while you dress, but you come out and get rid of her. Fast. We are going to talk, whether you like it or not."

"We've nothing to say," Leigh said.

"I have plenty to say, and I expect plenty of answers."

Leigh sighed as she watched his broad-shouldered form leave the room. If there were any chance — even the slightest chance — that he would believe anything that she had to say, she would be happy to talk to him. But Richard had done his undermining well, and her own foolishness in dealing with the night in Atlanta seemed sound proof of all that he'd had to say.

If circumstances were not in her favor that morning, they were definitely against her as the afternoon rolled by. She found Sherry and Derek in the kitchen when she had dressed, discussing the aftereffects of the recent storm. Sherry, she could see, was having a rough time keeping her hands off Derek.

"Leigh!" Pretty blond Sherry greeted her friend with a little hug. "I missed you!"

"I wasn't gone that long," Leigh replied wryly.

"But it seemed like forever!" Sherry exclaimed, flipping a piece of bacon, which caused Leigh to survey the cute little domestic scene going on around her. Derek was eyeing the toast and spooning butter over eggs. He was next to Sherry, brushing against her often with apparent comfort.

Just like Richard! Leigh thought painfully. Happy and at ease with anyone attractive and female while demanding everything from her. Her heart constricted and hardened. Well, Derek could play his games, he could extract his revenge, but he would never have a kind word from her, never draw an admittance of any feeling except total disdain!

Leigh sauntered farther into the kitchen and hoisted herself onto the counter. "Forever?" she queried with amusement. "You must have had very dull days!"

"Not at all!" Sherry chuckled. "We had a super beach party. Everyone was there! Except you, of course. Poor Lyle was so upset! He was astounded that you took off for a trip without telling him!"

Leigh winced as Derek's head jerked upward and he turned to her with questioning eyes and an "ah-hah!" expression. Yet when he spoke, his tone was amused and nonchalant.

"Who is poor Lyle?"

"One of our resident artists," Sherry responded quickly, draining the bacon on a paper towel. "Hopelessly enamored of Leigh. He has been for years."

Leigh's fingers curled over the counter. She felt like a drowning woman with no sign of help in sight. Yes, Lyle had a crush on her, and yes, he had had one for years. But the gaunt young artist had also had a crush on Richard! He was respectful though, amusing and a friendly companion, a young man who liked to keep his love life a fantasy that appeared in his beautiful watercolors.

It would be impossible to explain Lyle to Derek, especially when she could see by Derek's grim features that he assumed Lyle to be the "island lover" of Richard's grievance.

The sunny kitchen had drawn strangely tense and silent, and Sherry, having no conception of what her innocent words had implied, looked between Leigh and Derek with confusion. Then she gave a startled whoop.

"The eggs, Derek! They're burning!"

Somehow, breakfast made it safely to the table. Sherry took over the conversation, amusing Derek with tales of the flighty types that made up their immediate circle of friends. There was Sandra, a prolific but unpublished poet, who wrote most of her ballads for the sea gulls; Herbert, an artist like Lyle who took great pleasure in painting pictures of sand; Shirley, who wrote terrible tragedies for the confession magazines; and Norma and Harold Grant, who chartered their fishing boat for an income but who mysteriously disappeared for months on end to travel the globe when the whim caught their fancy.

"In fact," Sherry said giddily, almost passing out with pleasure as Derek courteously lit her cigarette, "we're having another barbecue tonight down by the beach to hear the calypso singers. Why don't you two come?"

"And meet Sandra and Herbert and Lyle and the rest?" Derek inquired politely.

"Yes!" Sherry exclaimed. "I've been teasing about them really. They are very nice, normal people. I'm sure you'd enjoy them very much."

Derek contemplated her suggestion for a moment, then gave her his charming smile. "I'm afraid we won't be able to make it. We're going to go back to my place on Star Island tonight."

Leigh was so amazed by his sudden decision that she choked over her coffee. What had happened to his vacation plans? "I thought —" she began.

Derek interrupted her quickly and suavely. "We have an album to work on. I want it wrapped up by Christmas, and to do that we'll need every day from here out."

"Oh, Leigh!" Sherry said excitedly. "*You* are working on it too?"

"It's Leigh's album," Derek answered for her. "And we have to fit a wedding in somewhere."

Sherry's cup crashed into its saucer. "A wedding!" she shrieked. She looked from one to the other of them quickly, her eyes reproachful and almost hostile when they alighted on Leigh. "You two?" She was decidedly incredulous.

"Yes, us two."

Derek stared at Leigh, his lips twisted into a hard smile, his eyes daring her to dispute his announcement. He stood and came behind her chair to massage her shoulders with fingers that bit into her flesh. "We deserve one another, don't you think?"

It took Sherry several seconds to shut her mouth so that she could reply. "But I thought — I —"

"Yes?" The prompting was pleasant.

"No— nothing," Sherry stammered. She inhaled deeply on her cigarette. "I didn't think you got along particularly well."

Derek laughed and ran a finger along Leigh's cheek. "We get along very well." He chuckled insinuatingly. "When it counts."

Leigh despised the rush of blood that filled her face. She was hot and cold and furious. "Derek —"

"I'm so sorry, love." He feigned an apology. "I suppose you wanted to tell your friend yourself! Well, sweetheart, you got to tell Roger and the others, it seems only fair that I should be the first to tell someone." His hands tightened on her neck. "I guess Sherry will have to tell 'poor Lyle' and the rest of your island friends."

Sherry didn't stay much longer. Her hopes dashed where Derek was concerned, she began to look a little sick. Leigh was almost sorry for her. She determined to tell her the whole truth when Derek's masquerade ended — whenever that would be!

"Marvelous!" Leigh challenged hotly when she had shut the door on Sherry. "Just marvelous! How far do you plan to carry this — this absurd fiasco! Haven't you already gotten what you wanted? Aren't you satisfied yet?"

Derek appeared surprised by her burst of anger at first, then his features took on similar grim lines.

"I'll carry it all the way to the altar, love," he replied with quiet venom. "And I'll be sure the altar I carry it to is a good hundred miles away from 'poor Lyle.'"

Leigh didn't know whether to laugh or cry. When she opened her mouth, it was the first that came out — a hollow laugh, dry and bitter, verging on hysteria. "You're an idiot, Derek, an honest to God idiot! You told me a few days ago you'd never marry because of me, and now you're contemplating marrying me! Because I was such a rotten wife to Richard! What a deal you're making for yourself, Mallory. Are you seeking revenge on me, or on yourself?"

He walked to her slowly and cupped her chin in his hand. "Maybe both of us, love, maybe both of us." Then he walked past her and she heard him move into her bedroom.

She followed him to find him pulling clothing from her closet.

"What the hell are you doing?" she demanded.

"Getting your things," Derek said curtly. "You heard me earlier, we're going back to Star Island."

"You may be, I'm not."

"Oh, you're coming, Leigh," he replied, finishing with the closet and moving on to her dresser. "You're coming with me if I have to truss you up like a spitted deer and throw you in the car myself."

Leigh's mouth worked furiously as she searched for the right words to say. "You can't do this! You can't take me against my will! It's against the law!"

"Really? We'll see." He dragged two suitcases across the room and tossed them onto the bed. "Shall you pack or shall I?" As Leigh continued to stare at him speechlessly, he shrugged and began to stuff her clothing into the suitcases.

"This is all very interesting," she finally said coolly. "But tell me, Mr. Mallory, how do you plan to make me marry you? You can hardly spit a bride like a deer and walk down the aisle with her. And I will never marry you willingly. I will never go through another marriage like —"

"Your marriage with Richard?" Derek jeered.

"Yes, my marriage with Richard."

"That's right, love, you won't. I'm not Richard. But cheer up. If you manage to divorce me, you'll be twice as rich."

Leigh choked back laughter and sat on the bed to watch him. He was dead serious! She blinked back tears. There was nothing in the world she could desire more than a lifetime commitment to him. In her secret dreams she had prayed that Derek would one day discover that he loved her with all his heart, needed her like air to breathe, cherished her as she did him.

And now he was planning to make her his wife. But he didn't love, need, or cherish her. He simply wanted to make sure she had no other life. He would bring her to heel, dominate and overpower her. Then he would go about with his own life, traveling, staying out, seeing whomever else he so desired. *Just like Richard.*

But she had fallen out of love with Richard and his behavior had become bearable. Richard, after their whirlwind courtship when she had given her heart, had quickly proved himself to be an unprincipled liar, weak despite the front he showed the world.

There was no weakness in Derek Mallory. In twenty years he had never thrown a professional temper tantrum, never been accused of anything but a judicious and fair mind, never been attributed characteristics other than generosity, toleration, and dignity.

She would never fall out of love with Derek. And the pain would be forever unbearable. No, she couldn't marry him. Even as her pulses quickened at the thought and her heart pleaded that it was better to have a fraction of his time than nothing, her mind rebelled. He could force her to Star Island, but he could never make her say the words that would bind her to a life of neverending misery and despair.

"Are you ready?"

Leigh snapped into the present. "Now?"

"Yes, now," he barked impatiently. His eyes roamed over her half-prone position on the bed. "Unless that's an invitation?"

She scrambled up. "I — I have to write Maria a note. That is," she drawled tartly, "unless you've already told her we're leaving again?"

"Write your note. I'll be packing the car."

Leigh stalked into the kitchen and began to write her note to Maria, explaining that she would probably be gone for several weeks. She was in such a turmoil that the pen ripped through the paper and she had to start over. After she had done so, adding Derek's phone number in case the housekeeper should have difficulty finding it if necessary, she wrote out an advance check for the next month. Glancing at her wristwatch, she noticed that the procedure had taken her much longer than she had expected. She was surprised that Derek had not come after her to bully her into hurrying!

She moved into the living room but he wasn't there. A quick glance out the front door showed her that the Audi was packed, but there was no sign of Derek. Puzzled, she walked tentatively down the hall to her bedroom. The door to the room she had shared with Richard stood ajar. She paused and looked in.

Derek was standing very still by Richard's heavy oak desk. His eyes were clouded, seeing nothing, his face white beneath his tan. His strange appearance astounded Leigh so that she, too, stood still for several seconds, watching him. Then she called his name softly, but he didn't hear her.

"Derek!" she called again, more loudly. He started, like a man coming out of a trance, and turned slowly to her. "I'm ready," she said, softly again, unable to fathom the haunted air about him.

A tremor shot through him. He shook himself, as if to remove an unwanted and annoying insect. A faint smile curved his lips but did not reach his eyes. "Good. Did you get the music?"

"The music?" Leigh queried faintly.

"The music. Your rough drafts."

"No, I'll run up and get them now." But she didn't run. She watched him, completely puzzled and not at all sure he was all right. "What are you doing in here?" she finally asked.

"The phone . . ." he said vaguely. "I wanted to let James and Emma know that we were coming back."

Leigh didn't dispute him, yet his answer made no sense. There were phones all over the house. "I'll go on up and get the music then . . ." she said, backing out of the room.

"You don't come in here much, do you?" Derek asked suddenly.

"No, no I don't." Leigh's eyes moved over the room, taking in the queen-size water bed that Richard had adored, the

Florida pine paneling, the heavy Victorian dressers and desk. "No," she said again. "I moved my things out the day I heard about Richard's . . . accident. I haven't been in here since. Maria comes in to clean."

"Richard's things are still all here?"

Leigh wasn't sure if he were asking her a question or making a rhetorical statement. "I haven't touched anything of Richard's," she said. "I always tell myself I have to get to it but I never do."

Derek nodded as if her words had been the answer to a deep and mystifying puzzle. "Go on," he said gently, "get the music. I'll check the doors and be in the car."

Amazed and incredulous at his abrupt change of behavior, Leigh backed the rest of the way out of the room. She sprinted up the stairway to the studio where she kept her work, organized the composition and her scribbled pages of notes, bound them, and hurried on out to the car. Derek waited at the steering wheel, his eyes dark and pensive, strangely distant. They focused on her sadly as she hopped into the passenger seat.

"Leigh, you're right. I can't make you come to Star Island if you don't want to. I think your work should be published, but I have no right to force you to work on it. We can hire Samantha."

He wasn't taunting her in any way, Leigh saw. In the few minutes that she had spent wording her note, something had happened to change him drastically. But what? She wasn't sure that she liked his new solicitude and uncanny remoteness.

"I — I don't mind working with the group," she said stiffly.

Some emotion raced swiftly through his golden eyes, an emotion Leigh couldn't begin to understand. He turned the key in the ignition and stared straight ahead, his attention on the road.

They rode in silence for miles, neither thinking even to switch on the car radio to alleviate the stilted tension between them. Leigh finally remarked on the beauty of the endless water as they passed over the remarkable seven-mile bridge that spanned the lower islands. Derek responded with an absent yes, and Leigh gave up all attempts at conversation. She didn't speak again until they cleared the Keys and were coming upon the mainland and it wasn't by choice then. The rumblings in her stomach were becoming embarrassingly loud.

"Do you think we could stop to eat?" she asked hesitantly.

Once again Derek looked as if he had been snapped out of a trance.

"I'm sorry. We have gone hours without a meal. Will Durty Nelly's be all right?" he replied.

"Lovely."

Despite its disreputable name, Durty Nelly's was a particularly fine crab house. Derek and Leigh both ordered the specialty, crabs, and draft beers. When the waitress had bustled on her way, Derek watched Leigh's face, his soulsearching eyes oddly intent. Their beers arrived and he sipped his, lit two cigarettes and handed her one.

"I want you to know," he said in a cloud of smoke, "that I'm very sorry. About everything."

Leigh lowered her eyes nervously, unsure of how to relate to this new person. She inhaled, exhaled, and sipped her beer.

"I'm glad you've decided to work on the album," he continued. "You are a talented lady, and your light shouldn't be hidden under a bushel. But you won't be harassed anymore by me. It's reasonable that you stay at my house, but you're free to come and go as you choose. I'll introduce you to the dogs so that you won't have any trouble with them." He paused, sipped his beer again, and absently swiped at the long-gone mustache. He opened his mouth, closed it, and took another long swallow. "About last night . . ."

Leigh uttered a muffled protest and waved her hand. Her eyes were glued on her table mat; she couldn't raise them to meet his. His hand caught hers in the air and covered it on the table.

"No, Leigh," he said. "Listen to what I've got to say. I'm sorry about that too. Very sorry. I promise nothing like that will happen again either. I'd like to go into this as friends. Do you think we can?"

Leigh was speechless, her heart torn in two. That Derek was being unerringly kind, apologetic, and gentle was something that she should love. But what did it mean? Did he no longer want her? Had their evening together, the one that had brought her to a heavenly cloud despite everything, been nothing to him at all? Had he decided she was not worth pursuing? Not until this moment, not until his promise that he would leave her alone, did she realize that, whatever the bitterness, whatever the antagonism that raged between them, she wanted him desperately — on any terms. His vile temper was preferable to his total rejection.

"Leigh?" he prompted.

"Yes, yes we can be friends." She did not trust herself to look up yet and spoke to the table. She moistened her lips. She didn't dare ask him about his sudden change of heart yet; she would hope the opportunity came later when she was in better control. But maybe now he would answer a few of the questions that had plagued her since she first came to his house. "Will you tell me, though, why you invited me to Star Island? And did you have something to do with my car not starting?"

"I did nothing to your car," he said, "and I invited you to Star Island for two reasons. The first is the music. I'll only tell you the second reason if you'll give me an honest answer to one of my questions."

Pinpricks of fear were gathering at her neck. She knew he was going to ask her about Atlanta. She had to find a way to hedge him. Taking a sip of beer, she finally raised her eyes to his. "If you didn't damage my car, how did it happen that I was there with Lavinia White?"

"Lavinia had scheduled an interview with me before I was even sure that you were coming. If you remember, I wasn't responsible for your entering into the interview. I didn't lock you out of your room."

Leigh flushed slightly. "But you did call her with all the information about our supposed romance. You must have. The people we met at Pennekamp had already read all about it!"

Derek frowned, puzzled himself. "No, I didn't call her. But then, again, if you remember, I wasn't the one to make the first announcement about a marriage. You told John and Roger and the group —"

"But you know why I did that!" Leigh exclaimed.

"Do I?"

"Of course!" Leigh retorted, "I was calling your bluff!"

"Well" — he shrugged indifferently — "it doesn't matter. But I would assume one of the group spoke with Lavinia. Roger, probably. He usually handles most of our public relations. Now," his voice lowered and he stared into her eyes intently, my turn. "I want to know —"

"Here we are!" The waitress cheerfully swooped into the conversation by producing Leigh's steaming plate with a flourish and then Derek's. "Can I get you anything else for the moment?"

"No, no thank you," Derek replied, controlling his impatience. "Oh, yes, two more beers please."

"Certainly," the rosy-cheeked waitress replied. She was a heavyset lady of about forty. As she responded to Derek, she began to study him more thoroughly. "English, sir, are you?" she asked politely.

"Yes," Derek said shortly. It wasn't like him to be rude and Leigh could see he was wincing at his own behavior. He glanced to the woman and smiled. "I'm originally from Northumbria."

The waitress suddenly sucked in her breath and exclaimed, "La-di-da! I know who you are now. You looked so familiar! You're the singing star! Oh, if my daughter could see me here! But, oh, honey!" She chuckled. "What the young don't know! Her father and I spent many a night by a warm fireside with your music ourselves."

Her voice was growing louder and Derek was beginning to regret his decision to be polite. "Please!" he shushed her. "I am Derek Mallory, but it's not me you listen to, it's the group, the London Company. And, if you don't mind, I really don't want to be recognized."

"Oh, I'm so sorry. Of course." The waitress lowered her voice. "But would you do me a favor? Could I have an autograph —

for my daughter?"

Derek grinned more easily. "Get me a paper quietly," he promised. "And I'll sign all the autographs you want!"

"Thank you!" Flustered and happy, she hurried away.

Leigh plunged in quickly to keep him from getting to his question. "Now see," she whispered teasingly. "You were recognized and it wasn't my fault at all!"

He groaned. "No, it wasn't your fault. But you did cause the fiasco at Pennekamp."

"Yes."

"And you did pour coffee all over me."

"Not on purpose! Really!" They were laughing together, naturally. It was a wonderful feeling, one that relaxed Leigh. She continued thoughtlessly, "Besides, I didn't hurt you badly. You were just fine . . ." Her words trailed into a choked whisper and halted. Last night. You were just fine last night. That was what she had been about to say. But she didn't want to find out about last night. She didn't want to hear that she had been just another black cat in the dark, silver-streaked or not.

This time she could have kissed the waitress. The lady, who told them her name was June, descended upon the table with a pen and sheets of paper in the nick of time to save Leigh from struggling out of her awkward predicament. "One for Cindy, Marilyn, and Louisa, please," she whispered conspiratorially with a wink. "And a special one for June and Dirk, please."

"Surely." Derek set his cocktail fork down and agreeably made out the autographs. Leigh noticed that diners at nearby tables were beginning to watch them curiously.

"Perhaps we should get the check," she suggested, motioning with her eyes to explain her statement.

"Umm." He finished his last scrawl. "June, would you get our check, please?"

"Right away, Mr. Mallory."

It was easy to stall Derek then. They were both involved with finishing their food quickly. But they had a forty-five-minute drive still ahead of them.

"Ready?" Derek gulped the tail end of his beer.

"Yes," Leigh picked up her own beer and gulped down the remaining half a glass. She was plotting as she rose from the table.

"It's amazing how sleepy a good meal can make you," she yawned as they climbed back into the car.

"And liquor," Derek reminded her.

"Yeah, the beer," Leigh agreed, with another strenuous yawn. She curled into the seat. "I never have had a tolerance . . ."

"Leigh?"

Praying she was a good enough actress to carry off her charade, Leigh failed to respond. She kept her eyes closed as he repeated her name. Was it possible to fall asleep so quickly?

At any rate Derek didn't push her, and as the car rolled along the road, drowsiness began to overtake her in reality. She awoke with a true start to find that they were parked in front of the Star Island estate.

"We're here," Derek said, nudging her gently. "Can you make it, or shall I carry you?"

"No!" Leigh sprang up and opened her door. "No, I'm awake. I'm fine."

She tripped over the first step. Her faked nap turned real had left her groggy and disoriented. As she wavered for balance, Derek came behind her and scooped her into his arms as James appeared at the front door with a respectful, "Welcome home, sir."

"Thank you, James," Derek responded cheerfully. "Mrs. Tremayne fell asleep on me. I'll bring her up to her room. Will you bring in the bags, please? And tell Emma

I'd like a cup of coffee in my office."

Leigh nuzzled into his warm chest as he carried her up the stairway, absorbing the scent of him, straining to remember every wonder of him, the feel of his breath, the touch of his skin. Tears were pricking at her eyes again. She had the uncanny feeling that this would be the last time he ever held her in the gentle, imprisoning security of his arms.

He lay her softly on the bed in the room that was once more hers. "Go back to sleep," he whispered. "I'm going to get hold of the group so that we can start tomorrow and look over the sheets you've written."

For a moment he paused, looking down at her. Leigh felt that he was going to kiss her, and she longed for him to do so. But he didn't. He moved a stray lock of hair off her forehead, his fingers lingering tantalizingly. Then he spun quickly away.

Her door closed, then reopened. He stood in the doorway, glancing upon her prone body reflectively. "Leigh," he said quietly, "I want you to tell me one thing. I'll never bring it up again, I promise. But answer me now, and tell me the truth. *Was that you in Atlanta?*"

Thank God the room was dark. Leigh

winced and bit her lip. To subdue the tears in her voice she spoke harshly. "Yes. Yes, it was me. Now, can we drop it, please?"

Chapter Eight

"Stop!"

Derek's voice sounded stridently as the instruments that now crowded his studio discordantly quieted. "You're flat, Leigh, start concentrating!"

Leigh bit her lip and nodded. The others, she knew, were looking at her sympathetically, but no one was going to rush to her defense. This was their last rehearsal before moving into the recording studio, and if Derek was being harsh and nitpicky, well, it could only be expected with the grueling schedule he had set. Leigh also had to admit that her voice had gone flat and that she wasn't concentrating. They had been rehearsing ten hours a day for a month straight. Granted, Derek worked long into the night, hours after the rest of them had called it quits, revising, improving, tearing the original work apart until it was musically perfect.

"Roger, take it back to the beginning. One, two, three, four." He ran his fingers through his hair as Roger began the bars of slow drum beats that introduced the final song. Derek came in on lead guitar, Bobby on bass, and Shane on the keyboard, then the crystal tones of John's flute, a sign from Derek, and their harmonized voices, Leigh taking great care to keep hers high and clear.

The song ended with a repeat of the slow drum beats. On the last Roger threw his sticks in the air and shouted, "Whew! I'm for a drink! Anyone care to join me?"

"I surely will!" Shane replied, rising from his bench and stretching. He tensed his fingers and curled them. "John? Bobby? Leigh?"

Agreement followed all around. They began to troop out the door, Leigh escorted forward by Roger.

"Why isn't Derek coming?" she asked him. "We're done, right? What else can he be doing?"

Roger gave her a quick hug. "Don't worry about Derek, love, he's always like this when he's really into a project. He'll come out when he's ready. Tomorrow things will get better."

Leigh didn't think so. Since the night they had returned from the Keys, Derek had barely spoken to her except during rehearsal and that was usually to yell. In public he had been polite, solicitous, but even then, distant. Leigh lived in his house, slept not forty feet from him, but might as well have been living on another planet. The only meals he took with her were when the entire group ate together. Otherwise, he avoided her like the plague.

"What'll it be, Leigh?" Bobby, self-elected bartender for the night, demanded as he shuffled through Derek's game room liquor cabinet.

"A Coke!" Leigh smiled wanly. "Anything else and I'd crash over on my feet. How do you all stand this pace?"

"You get used to it." Shane chuckled, patting her shoulder in encouragement as she sank into a plump chair. He walked over to the corner phone, saying, " 'Scuse me. I have to call the home front."

"Damn!" Bobby muttered, producing Leigh's Coke. "I'd better do the same. I promised Tina to take her to dinner."

Leigh chatted idly with Roger and John while Bobby and Shane made their phone calls. She was comfortable with the group now, close. Every night they had spent an hour together talking like this, an hour that Roger described as the "wind-down."

"Oh, brother!" Bobby exclaimed with

disgust as he rejoined them and sank disheartened into the sofa. "As if Tina isn't annoyed already with this rehearsal schedule! Her mother has come down with the flu and can't sit with Lara for us." He grimaced. "No dinner out."

"Angie and I can take Lara," Shane offered.

"No, you can't, but thank you," Bobby replied, draining his Scotch swiftly. "Angie has her dance class tonight."

"I'm sure she won't mind skipping," Shane said.

"You're not going to ask her." Bobby smiled wanly. "She missed a class for us a few weeks ago."

"Don't you have a live-in housekeeper?" Leigh asked him.

"Mrs. Smikle is on vacation," Bobby responded tiredly. "And Tina is funny about Lara. There are only a few people she'll leave her with."

"Well, how about me?" Leigh queried. "I'm sure Tina would trust me! She knows I'm crazy about Lara."

"Leigh, the offer is great, but no. You're exhausted."

"I'm tired of rehearsing," Leigh agreed amiably. "But I'd love to take care of Lara! And she goes to bed in a few hours."

"Are you sure . . ." Bobby was trying to dissuade her with his words but his eyes leaped with pleasure.

"I'm positive!" Leigh stated firmly. "Call Tina back and tell her you're still going to dinner. I'll change and follow you now. I'm not sure I can find the house by myself."

"There's no need to do that."

Leigh's eyes shot to the doorway where Derek was entering. He rubbed the back of his neck tiredly as he approached the liquor cabinet and poured himself a liberal portion of gin and added a splash of tonic. "Bobby," he continued, "bring Lara over here with her portable crib. She can spend the night. Tina can come to the studio with you in the morning and pick her up." He eased himself into a recliner. "You and Tina can have a whole night alone."

"Gee . . ." Bobby muttered. "That sounds great. But are you two sure you want to do this? You haven't had much time alone yourselves."

Leigh winced and felt pink staining her cheeks. Bobby, as well as the rest of the group, assumed things were still good between Derek and Leigh. Nothing else had ever been said about their impending "marriage," by either of them. The group, knowing their leader as they did, took

Derek's often abrupt behavior toward Leigh as normal. He was, they believed, frenzied and harassed by the work load that fell his way.

"I promise you," Leigh said, controlling the note of bitterness and sarcasm that threatened her voice, "Derek and I would both love to have Lara."

"It's settled," Derek told Bobby. "Call Tina."

"Thank you, both. I really appreciate this. And one of these days" — he winked — "I might be able to reciprocate the favor."

Leigh felt her stomach lurch.

An hour later Lara arrived for the night and Bobby and Tina blissfully repeated their thanks and headed off for a romantic evening. Leigh took Lara into the game room, where she read the little girl stories and played pat-a-cake. She was heartily surprised when Derek chose to join them, followed by dignified James with a tray of steaming cocoa.

"Snack, ladies?" he inquired, folding his long legs Indian fashion and sinking to the floor beside them. He patted the loop rug. "Right here will be fine, James."

James knelt to the floor, his brittle old

bones creaking. "Sorry, old boy!" Derek chuckled, "I should have taken the tray myself."

Offended, James sniffed. Then his basilisk features actually crinkled into a smile. "I don't mind at all, sir." His smile became reproachful as he continued, "I could do this with considerably more grace, Mr. Mallory, if I were to have more opportunity in the field of catering to little people."

"James!" Derek groaned. "I have my mother to nag me about my lack of procreation, thank you."

"And Lord Mallory," James supplied.

"Yes, and Lord Mallory," Derek agreed. "Well, James," he snapped suddenly, "would you like to join us for cocoa? Or are you going to kneel there and stare at me like a mother hen all night."

"Certainly not, sir!" He rose to his feet with a huff. "I shall be in the kitchen, sir, playing gin rummy with Emma should you require my services."

Lara had scrambled her chubby little limbs to reach her plastic cup of cocoa. Now she called after him, "Thank you, James."

James bowed stiffly, the silly smile back on his face. "A pleasure, Mistress Welles, a great pleasure." He shot Derek a final, reproachful glare, sniffed again, and left them.

"So, Lara," Derek questioned the little girl, "are you enjoying your stay?" A twinkle lit his eyes as they gazed upon the child, but Leigh could see the signs of strain in his face. The thin lines that edged his mouth and eyes were deep, the fine angular cast of his face gaunt. Why did he drive himself so hard? Leigh wondered. She longed to stretch a hand to him and ease his tension with gentle fingers. But she didn't dare. What was going on was more than work, she was sure. Derek was purposely burying himself, and purposely keeping a distance from her.

Lara scrambled to her stubby legs with childish grace, throwing herself into Derek's arms, cocoa and all. "Wuv it, Uncle Derek, wuv it!" she proclaimed.

Derek grimaced as cocoa lapped onto his shirt. "Good, sweetheart. Finish your cocoa now, and have a cookie. We have to get you to bed or your mother will have our necks." He grinned at Leigh with a wink.

Crazy, Leigh thought, how her heart began to pound. He had proved he wanted nothing more to do with her. . . .

"Yes," she said lightly. "Finish up now, Lara, so we can get you into your pajamas."

Lara happily crunched an oatmeal cookie and drank her cocoa to the last drop. She giggled with hysterical delight when Derek swooped her into the air and tickled her tummy. Then Derek looked to Leigh questioningly. "Where is she going to sleep?"

"The crib is in my room," Leigh replied. "I wanted to be sure I'd hear her if she woke." She lifted her hands helplessly. "I was afraid in a different place she might be frightened."

"Okay, munchkin!" he told Lara, tossing her to a position on his shoulders. "Auntie Leigh's room it shall be."

Leigh followed the giggling pair up the stairway. In her room she delved into the bag Tina had packed for her daughter and found her pajamas and teddy bear. Derek waited while Leigh washed Lara, helped her brush her tiny teeth, and changed her into the rag-doll patterned footed sleeper. Then he took over, popping Lara high into the air, kissing her soundly, and tucking her in.

"Lull-by, Uncle Derek," Lara demanded sleepily as she hugged her teddy bear. "Lull-by, please?"

"Kiss Leigh good night, munchkin," Derek said, "then I'll do the umber of your choice. Maybe we'll do some harmony."

Leigh leaned over the crib to receive Lara's obedient kiss. Soft hands curled around her neck and she hugged the little girl warmly in return.

"Now, munchkin, your request?" Derek queried.

"One Daddy does," Lara mumbled.

Derek frowned for a moment, thinking. He chuckled. "You mean the one Uncle Shane taught your daddy?"

"Yeth!"

Derek gave Leigh a crooked grin. " 'An Irish Lullaby'," he explained. Although a native Londoner himself, Shane had Irish parentage like Leigh. "Join me. You must know it!"

Leigh did, and she was now used to harmonizing with Derek. They sang the song together, softly, for the child. Their voices rose beautifully, magically, in the night, and Leigh was suddenly overwhelmed by a sense of loss and sadness. This was all she had ever really wanted. A family. A child to love and care for, a man beside her to share that joy. But the child was not hers, nor the man. The man she longed so dearly to touch, the man who had proved himself sensitive and tender as well as proud and arrogant.

"Better than Daddy," Lara muttered to her teddy bear with closing eyes.

"But let's not tell him!" Derek chuckled. His voice dropped to a whisper. "G'night, princess." He inched away from the crib quietly. "Are you coming back down-stairs?" he asked Leigh softly.

She shook her head. Her emotions were frazzled. She didn't trust herself in Derek's company tonight. "I think I'll go to sleep myself," she whispered back. "I want to be wide awake at the studio. I'll be the only one with no idea of what I'm doing."

"Good night, then." Derek turned for the door. He hesitated for a second, his back to her. Then he went out.

Leigh shook misty tears from her eyes. Absurd, she thought, how easily tears formed in her eyes these days. It was the hectic pace she lived at, she told herself. She was always tired.

Moving stealthily about the room, she prepared for bed herself, changing into one of Derek's tailored shirts that she had claimed as her own. He had never asked for any of them back, and Leigh continued to wear them, drawing strange comfort when she donned them, like a teen-aged girl with a pathetic puppy-love crush.

It was a long time before she slept, and when she did, it seemed as if she were awakened immediately. Sniffling cries broke into her awareness and she lay confused at first. Another cry came and she bounded from the bed, instantly alert as she remembered that Lara was with her in the crib.

Leigh knew something was very wrong as soon as she gathered the little girl into her arms and carried her from the crib. Her skin was dry, and her body felt as warm as a furnace.

Panic gripped Leigh in a dark vise. She loved children, but knew so little about them! How ill was the child who clung to her so trustingly in her moaning misery?

Leigh couldn't wait, she couldn't take any chances. Tearing out of her room in bare feet, her warm human bundle still in her arms, she burst in on Derek, crawling onto his bed and shaking him as she called his name.

Thankfully, he woke quickly. After one arched-brow look of confusion, he sized up the situation easily by the terror in Leigh's eyes and the warmth of the flesh of her childish package.

"One moment," he told Leigh swiftly. "Let me get some pants on." Not in the least a hypocrite, he made no suggestion to Leigh that she leave or turn her head as he sprang from his bed to clothe himself. "Calm down," was all he told her, with an encouraging smile. "I'm sure Tina put some children's aspirin in her bag."

In seconds Derek was dressed. He led the way back to Leigh's room where he tore through the child's bag. "Here we are," he said cheerfully. "Let's get a little of this into her."

Leigh looked on tensely as Derek prodded Lara fully awake and she downed a measure of the liquid medicine. "We're going to get a nice, long drink of water now, okay?"

Lara nodded drowsily but dutifully drank the glass of water Derek gave her. Derek grinned at Leigh from his haunched position by the child.

"Just a little teething fever, I think. Molars." He picked up the child and lay her gently back into her crib. Leigh perched nervously at the foot of her bed, feeling helpless and inadequate as Derek competently handled the child.

"Are you sure she's okay?" Leigh asked anxiously in a whisper.

Derek joined her at the foot of the bed. "Pretty sure," he replied cheerfully. "We'll keep a watch on her. But I'll bet" — and his eyes twinkled kindly — "that her fever is down already. Go and see for yourself."

Leigh glanced at him with disbelief, then tiptoed toward the crib. She placed a hand upon Lara's forehead. Amazed to find it cool to her touch, she lightly clutched the little girl's hands. They too were cool and soft, no longer dry and burning. After readjusting the crib quilt, she returned to Derek, baffled.

"I don't understand!" she murmured in bewilderment. "Lara was so hot just moments ago!" Sitting again, she met his eyes. "How did you know? I mean, how did you know it was nothing serious?"

Derek chuckled softly and set a friendly arm around her shoulder. "No great talent, I assure you. It's just that I've been around since Lara was born and I've been through a number of minor catastrophes with Bobby and Tina. When she was an infant, we all panicked over everything!" He smiled ruefully. "Then we all began to learn a little about parenting. A teaspoon of aspirin and water can save you from a lot of unnecessary, middle-of-the-night hospital trips."

"Should we call Tina and Bobby?"

"No, I don't think so, not yet anyway. Let's let them have their night."

"Yes," Leigh echoed hollowly. "Let's let them have their night."

Something in the sad inflection of her voice reached Derek. "You'd better get back to sleep yourself, young lady, or else the Lady of the Lake *will* sound like a sick bullfrog tomorrow morning."

"I can't —" Leigh began to object, but Derek quickly silenced her.

"Lie down and close your eyes. I'll watch Lara. Here . . ." He pulled a pillow from the top of the bed and laid it across his lap. "Put your head so" — he demonstrated by gently maneuvering her onto his lap — "and you can watch her yourself until you drift off."

"But you need sleep more than I do!" Leigh exclaimed.

"I will go to sleep soon," he murmured.

Leigh wasn't about to argue further; she was afraid to move or even breathe and disturb the strange bond of tranquillity that had formed between them. Lara, she could see, was sleeping peacefully. She allowed her own eyes to flutter and close, aware that Derek was stroking her hair. Then she too fell asleep in a cocoon of borrowed happiness. Sleep led to dreaming, and in her dream she heard Derek's voice and he was saying marvelous things. *I love you, Leigh, God, how I love you!*

Lara, demanding exit from her crib, woke them both. "Up!" she shrilled imperiously. "Up! Uncle Derek."

"I'm up! I'm up!" he groaned. Uncoiling his length in a luxurious stretch, he ambled over and lifted Lara out. "How do you feel?"

"Starvin'!" Lara replied with wide eyes. "Starvin'!"

"Oh, you're always starvin'," Derek chuckled. "Let Leigh get you washed and dressed and then Emma will take you down to the kitchen." He scratched his chin while he gave a groggy Leigh a rueful, "Good morning." Sauntering for the door, he mumbled, "This shaving every day is for the birds. Better get moving, ladies. I'm off to shower and dress myself. We have to be out of here in ninety minutes." He raised his brows at Leigh to make sure she was awake and comprehending.

She had never felt more warmly drawn to him, more aware of the complex personality that made up the man, more attracted to his sensual virility. He stood in the doorway, reddish-gold hair tousled, eyes still lazy with sleep, deep bronze chest bared and hinting of the trim hips and powerful legs beneath the faded jeans below. A catch stuck in her throat, preventing her from speech, so she nodded. What was wrong with them? she wondered sadly. As enemies, they created hate but a marvelous passion. As friends, they could only come so close.

"See you downstairs." He closed the door behind him.

Leigh despondently dressed Lara and called Emma to take the child downstairs so that she might shower and dress herself. She lingered in the shower as long as she dared, donned a light knit dress for the still-warm fall weather, and rushed down the stairway for the dining room, determined not to be late.

Derek did not join her for breakfast. Emma told her that he had grabbed a cup of coffee and piece of toast earlier, then hurried out to see that their instruments were properly loaded in the company van to be moved to the studio. Lara, too, had already eaten and was with Derek.

Leigh absently ate an egg, a few strips of bacon, and toast, forcing herself to do so. She didn't want to become hungry later on company time.

"More coffee, dear?" Emma asked as she bustled about the room, her voice ringing cheerfully.

"No, thank you." Leigh smiled in return. She frowned and looked at the dark liquid in her cup. For some reason Emma's usually delicious fresh-perked coffee was tasting acid and bitter. "I wonder if I might bother you for a cup of tea instead?"

"No bother at all, dear." Emma whisked away her cup and returned quickly with a steaming pot of tea. "Are you feeling all right?"

Leigh grimaced ruefully. "Opening-night jitters, I guess. This will be my first day in a studio as a worker instead of an observer. Butterflies seem to be playing havoc with my insides."

"Oh, you'll get over it," Emma assured her sweetly. "Just ignore Derek's growl. It's always worse than the bite, you know."

"I suppose . . ." Leigh said vaguely. She drank her tea beneath Emma's benign eye, grateful that the mellow liquid, laced with milk and sugar, seemed to sit much better than the coffee. Then she thanked Emma and braced herself to meet Derek for their trip to the studio.

Recording, Leigh learned quickly, was a

perfectionist's dream. Mistakes could be rectified, and if she had found Derek "nitpicky" before, she now found him to be impossible. They did the same things over and over, and over again until Derek was satisfied. At least, she thought, they were working with tracks, which allowed for each instrument to be recorded separately. Her mistakes did not cause endless difficulty for the others in the group. Tracks also allowed more complex instrumentation. John played the guitar for one track, flute for another. Derek played guitar and harpsicord. Shane, drawing upon a much loved but seldom used talent, contributed the haunting cry of his bagpipes in several, specially planned and defined places.

"It's really amazing," Roger told her one day when they were both behind the glass booth, watching John record a flute segment. "When we have the completed project, we'll sound more like a symphony than a group of six. Of course, if we take the album on a concert tour now, we'll have to hire extra musicians."

Leigh smiled faintly. She didn't think there would ever be a concert tour. They had been recording now for a month. The strange night she had shared with Lara and

Derek might never have existed. He was distant again, barely aware of her being in his house. At the studio he was harsh, and even when he yelled at her these days he called her "Tremayne." The album, she knew, would be wrapped up within the next week. And then she would go home, alone this time.

"Tacos!" Bobby suddenly sauntered toward them with his happy. announcement of lunch. He set the large white cardboard box on an empty chair. "Dig in. We all have thirty minutes."

Leigh reached a slender hand for a taco and then withdrew it.

"What's the matter?" Bobby asked, crestfallen. "I thought you loved tacos!"

"I do!" Leigh promised him quickly. "I'm — I'm going to let them cool for a minute." She grinned brightly, but felt terribly uneasy. She did love tacos, but the spicy aroma of them had churned her stomach. She dismissed the unformed idea that floated on the outskirts of her mind and helped herself to a soda. "I heard we're breaking early today for a meeting," she said. "A meeting about what?"

"The album cover," Bobby told her, grimacing as his taco shell broke. "And title. Right now this thing is just 'Henry the

247

Eighth.' We have to decide if we want to stick with it or not. You get final judgment on that, Leigh. But as a group, we always toss ideas around."

"Believe me," Leigh chuckled, "I'm not averse to ideas! Besides," she added softly, "I hardly recognize my own work anymore. Derek has done so much with it!"

"That is Derek," Roger agreed. "He can change a weed to a rose, and should he get a rose, he can change it into an exquisite garden!"

"Thanks!" Leigh knew he was telling her that her work had been the rose. It was matter-of-fact with them that Derek had unlimited talent.

On Star Island that night they mused for over an hour before anyone came up with any concrete ideas suitable for the cover. Shane ghoulishly thought that a chopping block and ax against a pitch-black background would be perfect.

"The man was a monster," he said, in defense of his scoffed-at idea.

"True," Bobby agreed. "But we always appear on our covers. Why not a medieval scene. Period costumes and the like."

"Leigh?"

She was surprised to find that Derek had

spoken her name, drawing her into the discussion.

"Well, I —" she stammered, afraid to voice her suggestion lest it sound ridiculous. "I think we could combine the two ideas. As Shane says, the ax and block center. And then as Bobby says, we can be the background. The king and his retainers and a random wife."

They were all staring at her and a slow flush spread through her cheeks. "It was just an idea . . ." she said weakly.

"And all in favor yell 'aye'!" Bobby called. A hearty chorus echoed him and Leigh looked around at their smiling faces, amazed. Derek, she noticed, was smiling too.

"I'd like to stick with 'Henry the Eighth' for the title," Derek said, "and underneath, 'Loved to Death.' It will fit perfectly with the cover, and also advertise what will probably be the most popular song. Any other suggestions?"

There were none. Everything had been congenially resolved. As the guests trooped out, Leigh moved awkwardly toward the stairway. Being alone with Derek now left her tongue-tied.

"Have a drink with me, will you, Leigh?" he called as she reached the banister. "It's a beautiful night. I'd like to walk down to the dock and watch the stars for a while."

His invitation caught her mid-step and she almost tripped with the shock of it. Turning slowly, she composed her features to nonchalance. "If you like. It does seem to be a pleasant night."

Leigh was stiff and Derek relaxed as he casually put an arm around her waist and led her first to the game room, where he gallantly poured two glasses of wine, and then outside, past the pool and patio and out to the dock. They sat on the planks and sipped their wine while they watched the brilliant stars in the night sky play upon the water. Derek began to rub gentle fingers beneath the hair on Leigh's neck.

"I have to talk to you," he said softly.

She looked at him with tremulous eyes. His face was gentle, the line of his mouth curved. She felt herself lost in the golden-brown hue of his eyes, lost and frightened should she be misreading the tender concern she found in their depths.

He pulled her more closely to him. "What I have to say to you isn't going to be simple. There's a lot that you don't know, a lot that I have to rectify with myself. And it will take time. I don't want any interruptions, I don't want to be worried about schedules or broken strings on guitars. But in a few days we'll be all wrapped up. Will you bide with my temper till then? And then, will you listen to me with an open mind? Part of what I have to tell you is going to be painful, and you may have to adapt to it as I did."

Leigh stared at him and nodded, the commitment of her agreement evident in the shimmering tears that specked her lashes. He hadn't said that he loved her; he'd promised no future for them. She had simply to trust in her love, but that was enough. He had asked her to wait, and she would gladly wait forever.

They didn't speak anymore, but sat by the water contentedly together, feeling the soft ocean breeze, listening to the gentle lap of the tide. Surely, Leigh thought, had she died and gone to heaven she could not have been more blissful and secure.

The chill in the breeze slowly increased as the moon rose full above them. Leigh shuddered involuntarily and Derek immediately suggested they go back to the house. He kissed her lightly as they reached her door, but she couldn't let him go. Her arms curled tightly around his neck and she clung to him.

"Don't go," she whispered desperately.

She couldn't bear him to take away his wonderful warmth; leave when she had just found him.

"Leigh . . ." he began in a groan, holding her hands still. "I told you, there's so much you have to know. I have no right —"

"I don't care," she murmured in a choked cry to his chest. "I don't care. And I do know that it's right when we're together."

Whatever demons he fought, he was only human. In the blink of an eye the door crashed open and she was in his arms. He whispered her name over and over with a soft and yearning desire that echoed lovingly of emotion deeper than the spoken word.

Both meant to play love's old game, to tease and to torment. Yet neither could. Sprawled upon the bed, they fumbled with one another's clothing, ripping rather than removing. The month apart had been long, too long. When their clothes were shed, their arms immediately entwined, their lips met with insatiable, feverish hunger.

For a second Derek pulled back, and in that time his eyes devoured her. They were a flame within themselves, and as they quickly roamed over her, Leigh felt her flesh begin to heat. Then his eyes met hers.

They asked a mute question, which she answered with a strangled sigh, hurling herself back into his arms. Her thirst for him had to be quenched. She arched herself to him, relishing the feel of her soft breasts crushing into his chest, the grinding of their hips in instant and mutual need.

"Derek, my love," she pleaded.

He needed no further urging. "Oh, honey," he groaned, "you don't know what you do to me."

But she did. As he shifted to take her, she opened to him like a bursting sunrise, and they melded together like molten lead. They were an inferno, feasting as if starved, and the ultimate consummation of their love burned with a fire more fierce than the sun's and left them with a satisfaction and togetherness more thorough than the meeting of the sky and earth.

And as Leigh slept in the serenity of her lover's arms, she knew she would ask no more of life than the heaven he gave her.

Chapter Nine

Leigh slept fitfully through the night, waking often to assure herself that Derek was still there beside her. He was, of course, his limbs entangled with hers, his arms possessively around her. She awakened fully to the bright light of early morning to find herself still curled comfortably along his length, his easy breathing in her ear, his head resting gently upon the auburn pillow of her hair.

Derek awoke as she gently tried to free her hair. A slow, contented smile curved his lips and highlighted his lazy golden eyes. He stretched long fingers to caress her cheek. "Morning, love," he whispered softly.

"Morning," she replied, subduing a sob that suddenly choked in her throat. He couldn't really be hers. Not this golden giant who had sworn revenge with savage arrogance and then made her a prisoner of his heart while arousing undreamed of passions with his magnificent body. She clutched his hand and kissed it feverishly and rolled atop his deep bronze chest. "Oh, Derek . . ." she murmured into his neck. She almost said, "I love you," but the words caught on her tongue. Their relationship was so very fragile! Ghosts still lay between them, ghosts that could easily destroy them. Not just the tangible spirit of Richard, but the other clouds he had created . . . doubt, mistrust, and fear.

"What is it, Leigh?" Derek asked gently in return, stroking her hair in a comforting gesture. "Talk to me."

She shook her head. "Not yet. Just hold me."

He did, and then he made love to her, slowly, sweetly. And when she shuddered and lay happily content in his arms, he continued to caress lightly the silkiness of her skin with a tenderness that she knew belonged uniquely to her alone. She gave him a dazzling smile.

"Derek, I have to know what's going on," she said, secure in his arms. "Something happened the day we left my house — something that changed everything. I need to talk to you, Derek, but I need you to be honest with me too."

His cat eyes were drawing a film, a shield, closing off from her as she spoke. "Leigh —" he began.

"Don't!" she protested. "Don't shut me out! Can't you see! We've been doing just that to one another all this time. Trust me, at least this once. Whatever it is, I can handle it. I really can, when you're beside me."

Derek was no longer touching her. His hands were clasped behind his head and he stared up at the ceiling. "We have to be at the studio in less than two hours."

"A lot can be said in two hours." Leigh knew she was pushing him, but fear drove her on. She had thought she could wait, take whatever golden moments were theirs and cherish them for just that — beautiful spaces of time that could linger forever in memory.

But she couldn't. She was terrified of whatever it was that lurked in Derek's mind. Life had taught her the bitter lesson that love could turn sour, and if she stayed with Derek any longer, basking in the depth of emotion she felt for him, only to have it all snatched away, she would never survive the blow. Within her soul she would be a cripple. They had to straighten things out. She had to know that he loved her, and that his love was a commitment.

"We have a tendency to argue when we

talk," Derek finally said, still watching the ceiling.

"Damn!" Leigh muttered irritably. She was a nervous wreck and he was being completely evasive. "We can't go on not talking."

"You're already arguing."

"I'm not!" Leigh exploded.

Derek whipped around with a strange savagery and planted his weight over Leigh's with his fingers gripped into her shoulders and his golden gaze burning into hers. Tension worked tersely in his facial features and the veins corded and pulsed in the length of his neck. Leigh shivered; she had forgotten the power that he was composed of, the strength, determination, and will that lay coiled at all times within the sinewed frame she so loved.

"All right, Leigh," he enunciated crisply, "I'll talk. But you won't walk out if you don't like what I've got to say. We've made a commitment. It isn't on paper yet, and it isn't legally binding. But we've made it, and you know it as well as I do."

Leigh stared into flaming golden eyes and nodded blankly. He was saying things she wanted to hear; why was his voice so intense and frightening? Didn't he understand that all she needed to know was that he loved her and believed in her and wanted to spend the rest of his life with only her?

As abruptly as he had pounced upon her, he moved away. His movements were erratic as he paced about the room, totally unself-conscious of his nudity, and as splendid and regal as a golden god of ancient times.

"Richard didn't have an accident," he told her matter-of-factly. "He drove off that cliff on purpose. I talked to him the night before and I knew he was very upset about something. He kept mentioning 'her' and I naturally assumed he meant you. Then he started talking about the past. When we were kids growing up together. And he talked about meeting you and how the days we had spent with your dad by the sea had been the best in his life. He kept repeating over and over again that he had 'missed the boat somewhere.' "

Derek stopped his pacing and looked at Leigh. Her eyes were as round as saucers, her face frozen in shock. She had thought herself beyond pain from Richard, but she wasn't. He had killed himself. She hadn't seen what turmoil raged behind his cool aloofness; she hadn't been there when he really needed her. No matter what had gone on between them, she should have been able to help him.

"I told you this wouldn't be easy." Derek's harsh voice broke through her remorse and the terrible guilt that washed over her in waves of agony. "But hear me out." He drew a deep, ragged breath and turned to the window, unable to comfort her until he had finished. "I blamed you. I blamed myself for not realizing how depressed he was when we talked. His last request was that I watch out for you. I laughed it off. I told him that you were a survivor and that he would fall in love again. We had all been in and out of love a dozen times.

"He told me good-bye and thanks. The next thing I heard was that he was dead. I wanted to strangle you. He was more than my partner, more than my friend. He was my brother. All those years when we were kids, when parental love meant boarding schools and an unspared rod, Richard and I had each other."

Derek's tone went very soft. "We were both mesmerized when we met you coming from the ocean like an innocent Venus. Everything about you was fresh and wonderful. The love and respect in your home were totally alien to anything we had ever known. Richard was quick. I remember how awed you were when you realized who you were marrying. But it was he who had found something special, and he knew it. He just didn't know how to handle it."

Leigh allowed her dazed eyes to focus on Derek. He was watching her now, and his eyes held only compassion. None of it made sense. He said he wanted to kill her, then he said that she was special. She didn't understand, but she was too numb to care.

With an impatient oath Derek strode back across the room and gripped both her hands. "Dammit, Leigh! I told you this wasn't the time to go into all this and I'm making a terrible mess of it all. Listen to me! Pay attention to me! Now I've made you feel responsible and that's not the case. I'm trying to make you understand the things I felt and why I behaved the way I did."

"I'm listening," Leigh managed in a whisper.

"I loved you even when you were my best friend's wife. I knew I couldn't have you, so I set you up on a little pedestal. I could be your friend, and I could be near you. I never allowed myself to think about you and Richard in bed . . . in one another's arms. I told myself that one day I would find a woman like you, a woman I wanted to have my children, to live and grow with together, to shelter, to come to. You were perfection to me, your marriage heaven.

"When Richard began to tell me you were running around and wanted out, I couldn't accept it. I had to mask my feelings with hate and anger. After he died, I barely made the funeral. I swore I'd never see you again.

"Then came Atlanta. I wanted it to be you; I was afraid that it had been you. It was gnawing me apart and I had to find out." He ran a finger over her cheek, reverently tracing the fine lines as the timbre of his voice went deeper in a husky whisper. "And I had to have you again. I convinced myself that anything I did would be fair because you deserved whatever I could do for all that had happened to Richard. I knew that I could find a way to trap you if I could just get you here, and perversely, I really was interested in 'Henry the Eighth.' Then, when you came, I was a mess! I loved you, I hated you, I wanted you. It was almost a sickness. I needed to be close to you, to understand you, but I couldn't stop myself from striking out, and I couldn't let you go until I had come to terms with myself."

Leigh watched the strong tan fingers that were curled around her own. Derek was telling her that he loved her. She should be ecstatic. She knew now beyond a doubt that he wasn't another Richard, that his desire was also for the love and security of a total commitment that she craved.

But she wasn't ecstatic. She was chilled to the bone. Richard still lay between them, now more than ever. She had indirectly failed him and led to his suicide, and no matter what Derek said, in his heart he would never forgive her. She'd have to learn to forgive herself.

"Why are you telling me this now?" she asked thickly. "We haven't got a chance in the world —"

"I'm telling you now because you insisted!" Derek grated, dropping her hands to grip her chin and bring her lifeless eyes to his. "And you could help a bit! I'm botching this entire thing because you're not giving me a single response."

"What do I say? Yes, I didn't understand Richard's frame of mind and so I did nothing? What will that do? Nothing. We both have to learn to live with it —"

"That's the point I haven't gotten to yet.

You were not in the least responsible for Richard's actions. I know that for a fact, but even if I didn't, I would have realized by now that none of us can prevent a thing like that."

Leigh frowned, confused. "What?"

"Richard left a letter for me in his desk. You never found it because you never went through his things. I was in the room that day to look through his phone book — I had forgotten my own number because I never dial it — and I found the note. He knew before he left for the West Coast that he wouldn't return. He had a disease of the nervous system that would have slowly killed him, crippling him first, and he couldn't bear to die that way. He didn't want you to know. He said he had caused you enough pain and that you would be able to cope with an accident — an act of God — better than the truth."

The paralyzing dullness of shock suddenly receded from Leigh, and the floodgates of pain opened with a shudder and an agonized cry. "Oh, God! Derek! I didn't know. I didn't know! Why didn't he come to me? He knew that I still loved him . . . that I would have done anything . . . he could have come to me . . ."

"Leigh!" Derek's arms were around her;

they held her with infinite tenderness as she sobbed, her tears streaming into the mat of his chest. "Leigh, Richard did know those things. And he did love you — very much. It was that love that wanted to spare you any more grief. It's all in the letter. He said that you had already suffered enough because of him. When enough time had passed, he wanted you to know."

He held her for a good hour while she cried, soft tears for the brilliant young man she had loved and hated, for the waste of his life, for the depth of his love for her that he had shown in his way at the end.

Derek mourned with her. Old scars had been cut afresh, they were bleeding again. Yet now they could heal. In a strange way they had given Richard Tremayne back to one another.

Leigh's tears subsided and Derek gently wiped the dampness from her cheeks. "We go on from here," he said softly.

She nodded against his strength. "I know."

"I love you."

She nodded again.

"I'm still a bastard."

It was a strangled sound, but close to a chuckle. "I know."

"We're both going to make it — together."

The bedside phone rang shrilly and Derek automatically answered it, his eyes never leaving Leigh. He listened for a moment, then muttered, "Thanks, yes, we're coming." Replacing the receiver, he tilted Leigh's chin again. "Hey! You promised me you could handle this. I'm beside you, and I love you. Are you okay?"

"Yes." Leigh attempted to smile but her effort fell flat. "Yes, I'm fine."

"I can cancel the session," Derek offered, his eyes denoting his obvious concern over her lethargy.

"No . . . no," she said faintly.

"Then we have to go. That was James to tell us were running very late."

Leigh rose, feeling like a zombie. "I'll just hop in the shower."

Derek retrieved his jeans from where they had landed on the floor the night before and slid them over his long muscled legs. "I'll hop into my room then." He grimaced ruefully. "Tonight we'll pick a room and transfer all of our clothing into one spot."

Leigh tried for another smile. "Yes."

Derek walked over to her and enveloped her naked shoulders in his arms, relishing the silky touch of her feminine skin against his. His lips brushed her forehead. "You could say something now, after all I've poured out to you. Something like, 'I love you too.' "

Leigh stared at him, her eyes still saucer-size and glassy. "I do love you, Derek. I have for a long, long time."

"Did you love me in Atlanta?"

"Yes." Leigh buried her head into his chest and rubbed her cheek against the coarse red-gold hairs that tickled her nose, "But I didn't know it then."

Derek groaned and his frame tautened against hers; his flesh became warmer. "I have to get out of here. We're going to finish the tracks today, the pictures tomorrow, and then get out of here. I want you all to myself." He clutched her tightly to him, pulled away and made a hasty retreat.

Leigh walked into the shower, still dazed. What was wrong with her? she wondered. She was shocked by the circumstances surrounding Richard's death. That was natural. But Derek was right; she couldn't have changed anything. Still, it was as if a wound had been ripped back open. She had loved Richard; she had been his wife for three years. He should have come to her. Yet in the end he had chosen a strange type of nobility. He had shielded her from pain; he had even made a vague attempt to clear her of the accusations he had made.

She had told Derek that she could handle whatever troubled him. And she could. It was something else that was bothering her, something she couldn't quite define. There would be time, she told herself philosophically. The man she loved returned her feelings and they would have all the time in the world.

With Derek's determination behind them, they completed the final tracks by five o'clock. Derek had last-minute details to work out with the photographer so he sent Leigh home with Roger. "If I'm late, don't wait up. Tomorrow may be hectic."

Derek was late, very late, but Leigh couldn't sleep anyway. She prowled the house nervously, chiding herself for not settling down. In the last two days her world had made a marvelous turnabout. She should be as happy and as content as a bird.

"There's just so much we have left to discuss!" she told herself aloud. "Plans . . . more admissions and confessions . . ."

Gravel finally crunched in the driveway and Leigh knew that Derek had returned.

She raced across the marble to the door, eager to greet him now that she had gotten over her initial shock. She had been so cold that morning! And in between all the sadness he had had to relate he had also told her many wonderful things. He had loved her as long as she had loved him. . . .

The door swung open and Derek's cat-gold gaze brightened at the sight of her. She had showered and changed into a lingerie set of misty blue gauze, and his frank appraisal and sensuous smile told her that her efforts were approved of and appreciated.

"I told you not to wait up," he murmured after a deep kiss that stole the breath from both of them, "but I'm glad that you did."

"We have a lot of lost time to make up for!" Leigh answered, grinning as the now-familiar heat he could produce raced through her limbs. His trim hips instinctively wedged closer to hers, and color suffused her face at the sure proof against her abdomen that she could arouse him as easily as he could her.

"I'm all for making up for lost time!" he breathed to her earlobe, nibbling as he did so. His lips, growing more urgent and demanding as they traveled, moved erotically along her throat and on to the cleavage enticingly displayed by the negligee, Leigh let escape a sigh that might have been a purr as her body responded to his demands with loving skill. "We're standing in the hallway," she told him dreamily. "I think we should move. This little scene could seriously endanger James's sense of dignity should he awaken and stumble upon it."

Derek lifted his head and laughed, the deep sound that could captivate her a room away. Then she was in his arms and they were moving effortlessly up the stairway. "It's all real!" Leigh said softly, meeting his smoldering eyes.

"Forever," Derek replied. He walked on into his own room and they fell to the bed together. No longer the least bit shy or hesitant, Leigh began working at the buttons of his shirt, teasing him with flicking motions of her tongue each inch of the way.

"You are a vixen!" Derek accused, turning the tables as he ripped away the last button and pinned her to the bed. "Now I shall play the tormentor!" He laughed.

His assault on her senses was slow and complete, his own desire held carefully in check as he teased and tantalized every inch of her sleek skin, savoring the fragrant scent, tasting its sweetness, exploring its perfection. His teeth nipped and grazed over her earlobe, finding each little erogenous zone along her nape. The warmth of his breath alone sent thrilling chills flooding through her spine; his touch, purposely designed to torment with arousal and withdrawal, turned those chills to a current of charged electricity.

"I love you," he murmured, his mouth moving sensuously over her breast. "I'm in heaven when I'm with you. I shall never have my fill of you."

"I love you," Leigh panted in return, moaning deeply as his teeth locked over a highly sensitive nipple and rotated gently.

"Like that?" Derek demanded hoarsely.

"Ummmmmm," Leigh returned breathlessly. "I like everything that you do . . ." Her voice trailed away with a gasp and her fingers dug into his shoulders as his teeth raked gently down her rib cage to begin a new assault on the hollows of her hips.

"And how about that, my love?"

His query was little more than a choked stream of air, as was her answer, yet they both knew that their murmured words of love could elicit deeper and deeper passion.

Derek's voice suddenly took on a peculiar note, which faintly surprised Leigh, but she was cocooned within his realm of expert seduction and it was several seconds before his words registered in her mind.

"And you're all mine, my darling, all mine now. You will never have to look for love from another man again because I will always be there. I shall keep you so happily busy and satisfied you will never have the need . . ."

Leigh felt as if she had been doused in a tub of ice water.

"*What?*"

"Nothing, my love."

Leigh furiously sprang into a sitting position, knocking him aside as she did so.

"What the hell?" Derek demanded, staring at her stunned, his eyes narrowed dangerously.

Leigh didn't care. The green of her own hazel eyes was blazing like dark jade. "I want you to repeat what you just said."

"I don't even know what I just said!"

"Yes, you do!" Tears stung her lids; she knew what had bothered her from earlier in the morning. Derek still didn't believe *her*. He no longer blamed her for Richard, but he had Richard's own words to rely on. It was evident that he still thought her capable of shoddy affairs behind someone's back.

"Dammit, Leigh!" he muttered angrily. "You have to be the only woman in the world who can pick an argument in the middle of making love."

"I want to hear what you said — slowly and clearly."

"What difference does it make?"

"How can you say that?" Leigh sputtered. "You talk about commitments but you think the worst of me! Love is trust and . . . and credibility!"

"What are you talking about?" Derek demanded, growing steadily angrier. "I didn't say I didn't trust you!" He scowled darkly. Lifting his arms to her, he commanded, "Come back here!"

"Not when you think —"

"I don't think anything. What went on between you and Richard and whoever else doesn't matter. The past is over. You might have had every right to —"

"To what?" Leigh prompted icily.

"To seek whatever comfort you did elsewhere." Derek impatiently pushed her shoulders back to the bed and straddled her. "I love you. I don't care. We're beginning anew," he continued, his words a husky, mumbled whisper as he resumed his lovemaking, his tongue sliding over her lips and his hands caressing her torso.

"Derek, stop it!" Leigh insisted. She held herself rigid despite the pulsations of sensuous pleasure her body refused to deny. "Stop it!" But he wouldn't take her protestations seriously. She knew he thought she was playing a feminine game, saying no but meaning yes, wanting to be cajoled into submission.

"Stop —" His lips fell over hers, muffling out the words. Then he was slowly caressing her soft flesh, and she doubted that he would even notice she had pitted all her strength against him. . . .

Then, it didn't matter. He claimed her with sure, knowing expertise, seducing with each demanding thrust of satin, hurtling her along with him into the escalating whirlpool of magic that she no longer desired to deny.

But she could not glow in the aftermath of their mutual satiation, nor seek the comfort and security and contentment of the arms that attempted to hold her with their usual ease. Despite the yearning she felt to settle back and bask in the simple pleasure of her love, she pulled away from the man who would undoubtedly hold her heart for life.

He groaned. "What now?"

Trying with great difficulty to stay completely calm and voice her words softly, Leigh smoothed back her damp auburn hair and said, "You aren't paying any attention to me. You think going to bed solves any problem that pops up. I wanted to talk and you —"

"And I forced you to make love?" Derek raised a skeptical brow.

"No," Leigh said evenly, but she knew her temper was slipping. "I'm not a hypocrite — believe it or not. I love being with you, I love what you do to me, your touch, your scent, everything. You. But that's not enough. I know. You keep saying nothing matters, that the past is gone. But it matters to me, Derek. It matters very much that you trust me and believe what I say. How can we form any kind of a life together without those basics? I want to tell you —"

"I don't want to hear about the past!" Derek grated, interrupting her in a sharp command. "Damn! Can't we just let it rest?"

"No!" She had tried, Lord, she had really tried. Springing from the bed with a furious oath, she stalked for the door, so enraged she completely forgot her state of total undress. Pausing with her fingers clutched around the knob in a white-knuckled grip, she turned back to Derek. "If you think you can listen to me, Mr. Mallory, do it by tomorrow. If not, I'll be heading back to the Keys and 'poor Lyle' by nightfall."

Derek was silent for a moment and their eyes clashed in a battle of willpower. Leigh would not allow hers to fall.

"I don't like ultimatums," Derek finally said coldly. He turned his back on her and sank his head into his pillow.

Shaking with a mixture of rage, pain, and frustration, Leigh threw open the door and flounced into the hall. Suddenly realizing she was as naked as a nymph, she sped toward the door that led to her own room. It was highly improbable that anyone would be roaming the halls at such an hour, but she still felt ridiculous on top of everything else.

But shades of the past were indeed engulfing her. The door was locked.

"Impossible!" Leigh muttered. She rattled the knob again fruitlessly. The door refused to budge. Sinking to the floor, she berated herself for having inherited an Irish temperament that didn't allow room for common sense. When walking out on someone, it was wisest to do it clothed.

Trying not to think, she rose slowly, tilted her chin, and headed back for Derek's room. If she was lucky, she could slip in quietly and grab her negligee. . . .

But she wasn't lucky. Derek was no longer in the bed. He was standing by the window in his dressing gown, gazing down upon the moonlit lawn. His eyes turned to her as soon as she entered the room.

"Back already?" he drawled.

"Just for my clothes!" Leigh hissed, snatching the gown from the floor. "My door is locked," she snapped.

The sardonic brow raised. "Again?"

"Yes!"

"My, you do have problems with doors!"

"Only in this house," Leigh replied sweetly, "so I imagine I won't be worrying about it anymore." Hastily slipping back into the gown and trailing the robe over her shoulder, she smiled a sarcastic "good night" and spun for the door to make a regal exit.

"Where are you going?" Derek inquired politely.

"To find a couch."

"Don't be absurd," Derek sighed. "Sleep here."

"You don't listen —"

"And I thought you weren't a hypocrite. You've slept in my bed before — one more night isn't going to kill you."

"I —"

"No," Derek said softly, leaving the window to walk toward her with the quiet tread of a cat. He touched her cheek just briefly with a single finger. "I won't get into anything else tonight. We're both tired. Let's get some sleep."

Leigh was tired. It had been an incredibly long day, long and traumatic. Her lashes fluttered over her eyes and she fought the urge to cry. "All right, let's go to sleep."

"I thought you might see it my way." Derek chuckled.

Leigh was already crawling into bed, pulling tensely to the far side.

"That's the problem," she retorted bitterly. "You refuse to see *anything* my way!"

Derek doffed his robe and climbed beside her, encircling her protesting form and drawing her against his warmth. "You know, one of the first rules of marriage is never to sleep apart. I heard that from a wise old friend."

"We're not married, Derek, and I don't think it's a likely prospect for the future," Leigh said stiffly, but she was no longer fighting the comfort he offered. It might truly be their last night together. She had been a partner once in a marriage that lacked communication and understanding. Not even for Derek would she contemplate such a thing again.

He didn't answer and within minutes she found herself yawning. "By the way," she murmured drowsily, "who was the wise old friend who gave you advice on marriage?"

His arm tightened securely around her. "Your father," he whispered smugly.

Chapter Ten

A park in Coral Gables had been chosen for the picture-taking session. Acres of rolling green grass and high-arched, vine-covered pathways gave credence to a scene from the medieval days of jolly old England.

Derek was a terrific Henry VIII — with his costume, a fake beard, and generous padding, and his own imposing height, he could easily pass for a reincarnation of the arrogant king.

Roger was dressed as the Archbishop of Canterbury, Shane, John, and Bobby as various noblemen of the court.

Leigh was to portray Anne Boleyn, and as the day went on, she was sure Derek had chosen her role with malicious intent. She spent an hour of posing on her knees by his feet, beneath his royal foot on the chopping block, then tearfully clutching his robe abjectly begging for mercy.

Despite the fact that it was fall, the temperature readings were closing in on ninety. Dripping with the heat, Leigh found it harder and harder to keep her temper in check. Derek, she knew, although he seemed entirely nonchalant and easygoing to all other eyes, was still angry. She had warned him again that morning that she was leaving, and his attitude had infuriated her further. He seemed as if he just didn't care. Now he was taunting her, all prefaced with smiles, as if all were well between them and he was any teasingly tender lover.

"Just one more by the block, Leigh," Bernie, the potbellied photographer called out cheerfully. "Then we'll wrap it up."

Gritting her teeth, Leigh once more folded her hands in prayer over the block, her knees sore now from grinding into the dirt. She forced a smile as a young makeup man powdered perspiration from her nose. Derek strode into position behind her, the others took their places in the background.

"I know it's hot," Bernie apologized, pushing his glasses back up his sweat-slick nose. "So we'll hurry the best we can."

"Take your time," Derek responded pleasantly, leaning on a knee and wedging his foot farther into Leigh's back. "We want to get it right," he added, "and besides, I think Mrs. Tremayne looks rather nice on a chopping block."

"Someone should have assassinated the king!" Leigh retorted.

To the left of her Roger started chuckling. Damn men altogether! Leigh thought. Always sticking with one another. Roger knew something was up between them, but he didn't take her seriously either!

"Too bad the Tower of London isn't handy," Derek commented dryly. "We could have gotten a few nice shots of Leigh behind bars."

Leigh opened her mouth for a nasty retort, but this time it was the frazzled photographer who interrupted her. "You have to stop talking or I'll never get *this* shot!" he moaned.

Then the work was finally over. Derek asked the band to join them on Star Island for a "task completion" drink. "Love it!" Roger agreed, his eyes dancing merrily. Leigh smiled grimly. Company was not going to prevent her from driving off the island.

She had packed her bag that morning, so once she returned to the house — in Roger's car — all she had to do was change. But she didn't get a chance to change right away. Roger affectionately pulled her into the game room. "I know you're leaving," he told her. "Derek mentioned it this morning. But you have to have one drink with us." He swept his priestly hat from his head and playfully bowed. "After all, my dear Lady of the Lake, this is your venture we have just completed. You and Derek *are* the London Company now."

Leigh chuckled at his antics, still objecting. "No, Roger, I am now retiring from the London Company. And you all are the London Company. Every one of you is important. I've been the hanger-on."

"Today I shall not argue, Lady," Roger said gallantly. "We shall resume this ethical question on another occasion. Today is a victory. What can I get you to drink?"

"Oh . . . white wine, I guess," Leigh acquiesced. Sadness was slowly creeping through her. She would miss them all so much! In the last months she had learned to love the band and the work that they did. She was a part of their camaraderie, of their family.

And even more a part of Derek. She blinked as tears welled behind her eyelids. It would be so easy to give way and just stay — agree with Derek and be his wife on any terms.

But such a relationship couldn't last. By his attitude he was calling her an out-and-out liar. And he refused to listen to a word from her!

"Hail, hail, the gang's all here!" Bobby called, filing into the game room with John, Shane, and Derek behind him. "Break out the booze!"

"Too quick for you!" Roger laughed, throwing beers on the counter. "Leigh and I are already indulging!"

It was a happy party. Tina, Lara, and Angela appeared to join in the celebration and gleeful, gay conversation filled the room. Feeling as if she were amputating a part of her body, Leigh joined in with the fun for a while. Then she singled out Roger and kissed his cheek. "I have to go now, Roger," she said quietly. "Thanks for everything."

"For what?" Roger scoffed, giving her a brotherly kiss back. His eyes were still dancing away. "You're special to all of us, Lady, and very talented at that. And I have a strange feeling you won't be gone long."

Leigh smiled doubtfully and moved away. Unable to resist, she looked for Derek. He had removed the beard and padding, and looked much as Henry must have as a young king — tall, strong, impeccably noble. But he wasn't watching her. His warm eyes, sparkling with their golden glow of interest, were on Tina, who was telling him something with a great deal of animation. Leigh closed her eyes and forced herself to spin around toward the door and the road out of his life.

She was reaching for the knob when she was abruptly and literally swept off her feet. Stunned, she stared in Derek's eyes.

"You should have told me you were ready sooner, darling," he said complacently, twirling in another circle to stride easily with his burden for the patio doors. "Tell everyone good-bye. A nice wave will do."

"Derek, I don't know what kind of a stunt this is," Leigh hissed as she was jostled in his arms. "But you can put me down this instant."

"I will put you down in a moment," he promised. Raising his voice, he called, "Hey, Roger! Are the bags on the boat?"

"James just put them in," Roger called back jauntily.

They were passing through the crowd, and everyone was innocently smiling at them. Tina, Angela, Bobby, Shane, and John. All smiling and waving as she protested.

"Do something, someone!" Leigh wailed, astounded. "This man is abducting me!

He's taking me against my will. He's —"

They were out on the patio and Derek was moving calmly but swiftly down to the dock and the boat. Roger — Roger of all people! — trailed a few feet behind them.

"Don't be mad, Leigh," he pleaded, chuckling as he watched her angry features. "We really think we're looking after your best interests."

"Oooooooooh!" Leigh spat, before exploding into a stream of oaths. She squirmed and pounded at Derek uselessly. He merely shifted so that she hung ineffectually behind his back, her costume helping to keep her prisoner.

And on the dock, releasing the ties on the *Storm Haven*, was James. Staid James, proper James, grinning away. "Have a nice trip, Mr. Mallory, Mrs. Tremayne."

"I don't believe this!" Leigh moaned as Derek skillfully hopped onto the boat with her in his arms.

"Bon voyage!" Roger yelled. He and James stood waving like a mismatched Laurel and Hardy as the *Storm Haven* drifted from her berth.

"What now, Errol Flynn?" Leigh snapped from her ignominious position. "You can't hold me and drive the boat or maneuver the sails!"

"I'll leave the sails for a while and we'll motor," Derek replied evenly. "And yes — I can hold you and turn on an ignition and steer!"

He went on to prove that he could do so while Leigh sputtered away vigorously until she realized she was wasting her breath. Then she hung limply, gathering strength for the moment when he would have to set her down.

They were out of the channel by the time he finally did, miles from shore. Leigh clamped her lips on a threat that she could swim. Dusk was falling and the shimmering lights on the horizon, blending together in the distance, informed her clearly that she would be a fool to attempt such dramatic bravado as a dive overboard.

Derek was watching her, a smile twitching on the grim set of his lips as he read her thoughts like a large lettered book. Drawing a deep breath for a rush of abuse, Leigh exhaled instead. "Why?" she demanded simply. Lifting helpless hands, she repeated, "Why? Why the dramatics?"

"Because," Derek informed her, his hand on the helm and his eyes scanning the ocean, "I have my faults, and I've been wrong — we'll go into that later — but you have a very major problem. *You* think running away solves everything. I want you in a spot where you can't get mad and take off."

"I didn't just run away! I warned you —"

"What about last night? You get mad so you hop out of bed and go running out stark naked!"

"I came back."

"You had to," Derek acknowledged bitterly. Cutting the engine with a flick of his wrist, he nimbly brushed past her to the aft of the *Storm Haven* and cast the anchor overboard with a whistling swing. If the situation were not so tense, Leigh would have laughed. Henry VIII balancing perfectly by the jinny mast of a twentieth-century yacht.

He turned to stare at her, his form tall and proud against the violet-streaked sky of the dying day. "Get into the cabin and sit," he ordered her curtly. "You wanted to talk — we'll talk. But you're going to get to hear why I didn't want to listen to your version of anything that happened."

"My version!" Leigh exclaimed.

"Go on down!" Derek demanded. "I'll be right there. Oh — and make yourself useful. There's wine in the refrigerator; you should find it easily. It's a small galley."

Squaring her jaw and clutching her long skirts around her, Leigh carefully climbed the wooden ladder down to the cabin. It was dark, but by groping along the wall she found a switch that gently illuminated the galley and adjoining dining room-den. The sailboat, Leigh decided, fitted her captain well. The galley was compact but complete down to a dishwasher; the den area simple but tastefully elegant, pleasingly paneled in a dark wood and decorated with silver gray drapes and matching seat covers. Stooping to reach into the waist-high refrigerator, Leigh found that it had been stocked with more than wine. Carefully shelved were rows of meats, cheeses, fruits, and various other staples. Derek, it seemed, was prepared for a long voyage.

The sound of his feet upon the ladder informed her that he had joined her just as she finished pouring the wine into the chilled glasses she had found beside it. Ignoring her, he drew the drapes to allow a cooling sea breeze to waft into the cabin while he impatiently began to jerk pieces of the Henry VIII costume from his body until he was down to the tight form-fitting pants and the knee-high boots. As he strode back to Leigh, she could read the tension in his face and sense the extent of his anger from the tautness of the muscles that bunched across his back.

"What the hell are *you* mad about?" she demanded crossly. "I'm the one who has been abducted!"

Derek picked up both wineglasses and set them at the mahogany table that flanked the starboard side. Reaching into a cabinet, he extracted an ashtray and a pack of cigarettes. Sliding into the seat, he motioned her next to him. "Sit down. Start talking. I'm listening."

Nervously, Leigh took the seat he indicated. She took a swallow of her wine and accepted a light for a cigarette, growing increasingly uneasy beneath the relentless intensity of his dark glower. "Go on," he prompted.

"Tell me why you are angry, first," Leigh suggested hesitantly. She felt totally tongue-tied, at a loss. How could she carry on an intimate conversation when he was acting like a hangman?

"You'll understand in a few minutes," he sighed, seeming unwillingly touched by her confusion. "Start talking — I'll try to help."

Lamely, with broken words, Leigh tried to explain her relationship with Richard: how entranced she had been at first, then how shattered she had become when she realized that Richard had a woman waiting in every city and that she was simply supposed to accept the situation because he was Richard Tremayne. She told him about the constant temper tantrums toward the end, the mental cruelty he would purposely inflict. "I tried to talk to you about Richard then," Leigh said, watching the smoke curl into the air from the glowing tip of her cigarette. "I told Richard a month before I filed the papers that I intended to do so. But Richard had your ear, and he didn't believe I would divorce him. Not until he was served the papers." Forcing herself to meet Derek's eyes squarely, Leigh turned to him and said, "But not once, Derek, not once, no matter what was happening, did I ever see anyone else. I was too hurt and bewildered to chance an involvement. Richard had shattered all my beliefs in what marriage and love meant."

It was Derek who shuttered his gaze and turned away. A lock of reddish-gold hair fell over his forehead, hiding his lowered head completely. Leigh sat tensely watching him, surprised by his silent reaction. Suddenly the hand that held his wineglass rose and slammed back to the table, splintering the fine crystal into minuscule pieces and splaying wine in every direction. His focus turned to Leigh and there was rage and pain in the depths of his eyes, which had turned as dark as the mahogany table. "Why?" he exploded. "Why do you insist upon lying to me? I told you I didn't care — that I just didn't want to hear!"

"I'm not lying!" Leigh cried, frightened by his vehemence but more bewildered than ever and determined to cross the gulf between them. "Damn, Derek!" she pleaded, resisting the temptation to touch him by clenching her nails into her palms. "You tell me that you love me, but you won't even give me the benefit of doubt! You tell me why! Why are you so convinced that Richard's lies about me were the truth?"

"Because I have it in black and white," Derek said, his voice low and strained.

"What?" Leigh's whisper was a breath of utter disbelief.

"The letter, Leigh. The rest of Richard's letter. It's a damn deathbed confession! He wouldn't have lied to me in that; he wanted me to watch out for you." Shreds of glass covered Derek's hands but he didn't notice. A pool of wine lay over the table, but neither suggested they mop it up.

"I don't believe that either, Derek," Leigh choked sickly. "He wouldn't purposely have lied . . . then."

"God, Leigh," Derek groaned, "don't you see that I do believe in you? I understand how rotten things were for you — Richard did like to play the 'star.' I don't condemn you for anything. But I don't want to start our life with lies, either. We just drop it — whatever was was."

Feeling like a broken record Leigh dropped her forehead into the palm of her hand and repeated, "But I'm not lying!" Lifting her head with sudden inspiration, she asked, "Do you have the letter?"

"Yes, why?"

"Because I may find something in it you didn't!"

Derek shrugged as if the effort was useless, but he rose and disappeared into the forward cabin. Leigh picked up the broken glass while he was gone and searched the cabinets for another. When Derek returned, she had cleaned the table and set the new glass at his place. The little task had kept her from climbing the sailboat's walls.

The letter had been in his wallet, and as Derek pulled it out and handed it to Leigh, she could see the crease marks. He must have read it and replaced and reread it a hundred times.

Leigh glanced at his heavy countenance once, then turned her full attention to the words before her in Richard's sprawling script. The sight of his handwriting alone caused a constriction of sadness to form in her throat, but she had to read the letter. Knowing the fullness of his concern for her at the end, she couldn't believe that he would purposely malign her.

The letter was short, just two paragraphs and a line. The first dealt with his knowledge of his disease and his decision to end it all his own way, which Derek had already told her. Everything Derek had said was true; without going into detail, Richard admitted sadly that he had hurt her. His written word begged that she be spared as much further grief as possible.

It was the second paragraph that unwittingly condemned her:

I don't think Leigh realizes the depth of her own feelings, but she has been in love with a great guy for a long time. I've seen it; I knew it from the very start I suppose, but, well, being me, I just couldn't let her go. A real noble man. Ha-ha. Sorry — you know my bloody sense of humor. Maybe I am a little bitter. Seems like I'm the one that has to go. It was life, and I lived it. My only regret is Leigh. She deserved him in the first place. I hope that she gets more than stolen moments now. See to it, long-time friend and brother, will you?

Good luck, health, and long life to you both.

Leigh read the paragraph and parting line three times; she choked, sobbed, then began to laugh. It was a sad laugh, one that verged on hysteria. Looking from the paper with tear-bright eyes, she met Derek's pained and incredulous stare. It was obvious that he thought she had plummeted over the brink and become totally demented.

"Oh, don't you see? You mammoth idiot! To the music world, Derek, you may be a genius, but you can be as dense as a forest full of trees!" Leigh exclaimed, smiling ruefully through her tears. "Richard is talking about *you*. He understood our feelings before either of us did — before either of us could ever admit such a thing!"

Derek was still staring at her stunned. " 'A noble man,' " Leigh quoted. "Nobleman — dear future Lord Mallory. Richard was far more perceptive than I ever would have imagined. 'Good luck, health, and long life to you both.' This letter does more than ask you to look out for me, it's Richard's blessing. He wanted us to be happy together!"

Derek grabbed the sheet from her hand and his eyes scanned the paper. After a moment he dropped the worn sheet and unraveled his length to walk tiredly to the ladder and lean against it, his face pressed to the cold wood. Oh, God! Leigh thought desperately, he still doesn't believe!

She sat staring at him, in a trance of fear. The world and time stood still; she didn't dare think or even breathe. Lord, why didn't he say something? Didn't he know that she couldn't bear his terrible withdrawal one second longer?

"Derek!" she cried, her calling of his name ripped from her throat in a pathetic screech of agony. It was a beseechment from the soul that would have shattered a heart of stone.

He came back to her then and knelt at her feet, his hands and the tremendously long and powerful fingers that were music themselves locked more tenderly over hers than ever they had graced a keyboard. Tentatively, Leigh withdrew one hand and gently set her own delicate fingers upon the crisp reddish-gold hair of the head bowed over her lap.

"Oh, Lord, Leigh! I couldn't see what was right before my own bloody eyes! I was so afraid . . ." His voice was broken and cracking; his explanation trailed into a groan. "Can you ever forgive me, my dearest love?"

"Forgive you?" Leigh gasped, still trying to assimilate the fact that he was on his knees before her and that their ghosts had finally been laid to rest. For a brief moment she thought of Richard, and she thanked his fading spirit with a silent tear. Then she freed her other hand to clutch it too into the golden curls before her and lift Derek's head so that she could meet his golden eyes. All shadow of doubt was gone. In his gaze she found a wealth of unspoken eloquence, and she knew he offered her everything she had ever desired — not only undying love and devotion, but the complete belief and trust that would allow that love to grow to endless bounds for all the days of their lives. A smile of sheer relief and happiness stretched its way into her eyes, adding the beauty of radiance to the loveliness of her finely chiseled features.

"Forgive you?" she repeated incredulously. "My dear, dear Lord Mallory. I forgive you with all my heart! And I will love you with all my soul and being well into eternity!"

She planted a kiss of infinite tenderness upon his brow, then a spark of mischief lit her eyes and she began to chuckle softly. "Now get off your knees, Lord Mallory!" she commanded. "Your female fan club wouldn't like this one bit!"

"My female fan club can go hang!" Derek declared, slowly grinning. "I seek the approval of only one female in the entire world." He started to rise, but lowered himself back down, a definitely roguish expression settling into his rugged profile. Her chuckle became a knowing laugh, she had never expected her arrogant lover to remain humble for long.

"Hush, woman!" he ordered. "I decided to say one more thing while I'm down here. It's highly unlikely you'll ever get me into this position again!"

Leigh raised impudent brows. "Speak, my lord!"

"This is a proper proposal. Will you marry me?"

"You'll never get out of it!" Leigh vowed. "When?"

"As soon as we can get a license. I'd like to fly to Georgia and spend my wedding night and honeymoon in a certain house on a hill near Atlanta. I was seduced there once by a fantasy witch, a woman from a dream." Derek pounced gracefully to his feet and pulled Leigh up beside him as he whispered on in her ear. "She was a real vixen, but I fell in love with her then and there and I would have spent my life searching for her." Running his tongue over her earlobe and tracing a pattern of erotic little kisses along her throat, he murmured, "I wonder if she likes to make love on boats. It's a delightful experience beneath the stars . . ."

"I'm sure she'd adore it," Leigh panted, gasping for the breath he was robbing from her lungs. "She is, you know . . ."

"My lady," Derek murmured. "Always."

Somehow, Derek managed to keep his mouth tantalizing her skin while he slid the draping "Boleyn" sleeves from her arms. Then he found himself stumped. "Where's the zipper on this damn thing?" he quizzed, annoyed and impatient.

Leigh smiled seductively and very slowly started to work apart the tiny hooks that held the costume together. "They didn't have zippers in the sixteenth century," she told him innocently. "You rented from an authentic costume shop." Shimmying from the dress seductively, Leigh gave him a wicked smile and bolted up the ladder. Beneath the moon she cast aside the remainder of her flimsy undergarments, knowing that he watched her, knowing his eyes were glittering gold with desire. . . .

Derek reached for her and she turned impishly to throw herself into his arms, only to slide down his length and help him out of the high boots. She watched him with frank feminine approval as he slid out of the tight pants, then waited as he came for her. Their bed was a spot beneath the proud mainmast; their ceiling the star-blanketed sky. The harmony of their voices was that of their bodies and souls as they came together, satisfied for a timeless moment to touch, arms wrapped tenderly around one another, her breasts crushed against the crisp hair of his chest, her hips pressed to his, her long, slender legs inter-woven with his longer, more powerful ones.

And yet that moment, beautiful in itself and meant to be cherished, could not, of its own making, last. Still, it was a portent of things to come. Simultaneously, they sank to their knees together, and Derek reverently kissed the palm of her hand and each finger before claiming the sweetness of her mouth.

Tonight was new again, tonight the bonds of their love would be irrevocably sealed beneath the heavens.

Leigh shivered as the intensity of his kiss brought them down together and the easy roll of the *Storm Haven* abetted the rising desire between them. Their tongues did not duel, but sought deeper in demand, until Derek's muffled cry brought them apart, only so that his lips could taste more of her. Tenderly, feverishly, then tenderly again, his lips traveled her flesh, savoring her throat, her breasts turned hard with longing, her stomach, which constricted at his touch, her quivering thighs, her knees, her toes . . . everything; he was compelled to know every inch of her. . . .

And Leigh trembled with the burning sensations of his loving desire, certain that they had become one with the stars as she was consumed bit by bit, as if little flames licked at her, until she could no longer endure the exquisite torture. Crying out for him, she threw her arms out in beseechment, then drew him back to her. Even as he began the culmination of her deliciously agonized longing, she was tasting the salt sea mist of his lips again, grazing her teeth over the satin-smooth tightness of his shoulders, allowing her hands the possessive appeasement of following the sturdy line of his powerful back, her fingers the return enticement of curling into the mat of his chest, of teasing along his ribs. . . .

The mounting cloud of desire that only they could elicit in one another raged until it became a passionate storm that swept away all else. The world itself was eradicated; there were only the two of them, one body, one soul. A beautiful, synchronized harmony that was a love song soaring ever higher with each rhythmic, combustible beat . . .

And a crescendo of sweet, sweet, exquisite ecstasy. One that left them both satiated to the brim with awe and quaking contentment, loathe to break their entwinement in any way.

Leigh sighed happily and half opened sensuously lazy eyes to the sky. It was with wonder that she realized her fantasy had finally become real, unquestionable and complete. She moved finally to touch the damp tendrils of hair that lay upon her chest. She would always need to touch him.

And he her.

He shifted as she moved, but only to look at her with a knowing smile, and rearrange their positions to place protectively his heavier form against the deck and pull her into the comfort of his shoulder. Neither was really ready to stir yet; they were basking in the blissful, semiconscious state of euphoria that followed such a bout of fully committed and hungrily passionate lovemaking.

Leigh's lids began to droop and her lashes brushed softly against her cheeks. The timeless sensation was still with her, an enveloping feeling of happiness and security with Derek beside her, holding her. She slept, knowing they had forever.

Later, Leigh stirred in her lover's arm and wedged closer for warmth. The moon was high above them in the heavens and the sea breeze chilled the dampness of her contented form.

"Cold?" Derek murmured.

"A little."

"No romance!" Derek grumbled, encircling her closer. "You're supposed to say something like, 'Not with you to warm me!' I am a hot thing to handle, you know."

"Oh, I'd be the last to deny it, believe me." Leigh laughed. "But maybe you could be 'hot' down in your cabin."

"Anywhere you like." Derek started to rise but Leigh stopped him with a wistful smile.

"In just a minute. I want to watch the stars a bit longer."

Sliding his arms around the back of her shoulders, Derek sat, his thumb lovingly brushing her cheek while she cradled her head against his shoulders. "I have another confession to make anyway," Derek said. "So I might as well tell you here. If you decide to jump out of bed on me, you'll wind up in the Atlantic."

"*Another* confession?"

"Umm . . . I played a trick on you last night, but my intentions were the best. I didn't want you getting away. When you pulled your streaking act out of the room, I slipped through the adjoining door and locked yours."

"You didn't!"

"I did. I couldn't bear the thought of going to sleep without you after I had you in my arms again."

"I didn't even know there was an adjoining door! Why you son of a —"

"Hey!" Derek growled teasingly. "Don't you dare say it! My mother is a nice woman and she bears absolutely no resemblance to the canine family."

"I was going to say son of a gun," Leigh protested.

"Nothing metallic in the family line either. But while we're on it" — his voice abruptly grew low and gently serious — "how do you feel about a son?"

"I'd like one very much, but they don't come by order. We could have a daughter," Leigh advised him.

"We can keep trying until I we have one of each," Derek mused.

"That sounds terrific," Leigh sighed.

Derek's touch on her chin intensified and he twisted his head to face her. "Really, Leigh, would you mind if we started a family quickly? We have everything to give children, a secure future, a good home, and most important — love."

Leigh crossed a leg and rose gracefully to her feet. The *Storm Haven* swayed beneath her as she placed a slender hand in Derek's and drew him to her. God, how she loved him!

Her hair fell over her shoulders in deep rippling red, curling around her breasts; her eyes gleamed with the devilry of the full moon.

"Quickly?" she queried impishly, giving him her best vixen smile. Yes, quickly. This man of hers did have everything, strength, dignity, love, and compassion. He would make a wonderful parent.

In one fluid motion she came to her feet and stretched out her hand wordlessly, telling him all he wished to know.

Epilogue

She had known him for years, yet each day was a voyage of new love and discovery. She was his best friend, his partner, his lover, his mistress, his wife.

And it was a special night. A secret anniversary.

She had wanted him forever, loved him for an eternity.

He was a pirate tonight, a swashbuckling pirate with a rakish air and devilish smile. She was a gypsy, flamboyant and colorful, promising heavenly delight with boldly flirtatious, glittering hazel eyes.

But it didn't matter what their guises. She loved him as a king, as a pirate, as her lordly mate, Derek Mallory.

And he knew exactly who she was. He loved her for exactly who she was, and for all the complexities that were what she was.

His eyes met hers across the room, then swept slowly over her figure with astute appreciation. Before she knew it she was in his arms. It felt so good, so right. He was everything wonderful: tall, strong, arrogantly masculine, and yet unceasingly tender. They belonged to one another as only very special lovers ever could.

He suggested that they leave and she didn't blink an eye. Her slow, suggestive smile was all the answer he needed.

She vaguely noted that a leprechaun and a well-feathered Indian were discussing the London Company as they neared the pair, extolling the virtues of the group's latest album.

"Leigh, Derek!" the Indian joyfully exclaimed. "I was just telling John about the calls I've had. The movie companies are hounding me! Do you believe that? Lord!" he said with a chuckle, "if I do say so myself, with the team of Mallory and Mallory in the lead of the London Company, we surpass genius!"

John, the leprechaun, smiled wryly. "Nothing like patting ourselves on the back!"

"Seriously," Roger groaned, adjusting a loose feather, "what answers do I give these people?"

"Whatever you want," Derek told him, his eyes on his wife. "Just don't commit us to anything until next month. Lord and

Lady Mallory have descended upon South Florida to care for their grandson and Leigh and I are leaving for the next four weeks."

"Where —" Roger began.

"Oh, no!" Leigh exclaimed with a smile. "No one knows where we're going! We don't want to be found."

"I'm sure you'll handle whatever comes up, Roger," Derek said patiently. "John, thanks for a super party. Have a good vacation too."

"You two are going now? It's early!"

"We are, indeed, leaving," Leigh chuckled, tucking her hand into her husband's crooked arm. "Why don't you two run over and flirt with Sherry? This is her first big party and she is crazy about musicians!"

They were watched as they left. They were a fantasy couple: both tall, graceful, handsome, enviably in love. Happiness radiated from them and encompassed all who came near.

So began their special night. It was slow and easy and wonderful. They listened to the gentle strains of classical music as they sipped on mulled wine before the light and warmth of a mellow fire. They talked for hours, about their music, their friends, their son, the silken fantasy of their lives.

Their talking tapered into comfortable silence. He rose slowly and offered her his hand. By mute agreement she trustingly accepted him, and when she, too, was standing, he swept her as effortlessly as stardust into his arms and lay her tenderly on the bed, where he disrobed her with loving reverence. She was naked now, susceptible and vulnerable. But his love was her strength, his powerful arms her harbor. And as always, she was lost in an endless field of longing and desire, totally absorbed in the magnificent male form before her, framed in a silhouette by the fire like a true golden king.

"With my body I thee worship," he whispered, his husky voice, against her throat sparking the fire that would soon rage through her veins and consume them.

Her fingers locked into his hair as their forms melded together. Lips played upon flesh, hands teased and caressed provocatively. Even as Leigh responded to her lover's whispers of hunger and desire, she knew that they were blessed with the one ingredient for everlasting passion. Love. Then the fire raged out of control, and she no longer thought but surrendered to the ecstasy that enveloped and overwhelmed her. He demanded, he took, he gave, and all through the long night he proved once more that he would never have his fill of her.

Too soon the dawn broke across the heavens. She awoke with a start to find herself entwined with him, her head resting on his golden chest. She smiled with sweet fulfillment and joy, then carefully, so as not to awaken her sleeping king, she disengaged herself and dressed. She scampered to the door, but stopped. She had to go back, just for a second, just to kiss his sleep-eased brow.

Her lips touched his skin, then she backed away. His eyes were beginning to flicker. She made it to the door before he awoke and called for her to stop, demanded to know where she was going.

"For coffee!" She chuckled ruefully. "I thought I could make it back before you awoke and surprise you."

"That's okay." He leaned on an elbow to watch her with contented, lazy eyes that still sparkled golden with insinuation. "You can go."

"Oh?" She raised teasing brows. "And what if I disappear?"

He rose from the bed and sauntered toward her. "You will never disappear, love." He kissed her until she went limp against him, weak and breathless. "You are truly part of me now." He drew her closer to him, his embrace promising that they would be together forever.

The employees of Thorndike Press hope you have enjoyed this Large Print book. All our Large Print titles are designed for easy reading, and all our books are made to last. Other Thorndike Press Large Print books are available at your library, through selected bookstores, or directly from the publishers.

For more information about titles, please call:

(800) 257-5157

To share your comments, please write:

Publisher
Thorndike Press
P.O. Box 159
Thorndike, Maine 04986